<u>Mac Ireland</u>
Fight for Irish Freedom

Published by Mac Ireland Publications

P.O. Box 15128

Washington, D.C. 20003-0849

SeanMcManus6@mac.com

ISBN-13: 978-1484909379

ISBN-10: 1484909372

CreateSpace, North Charleston, SC

Cover design: Barbara J. Flaherty

DRAMATIS PERSONAE

(Characters in the book)

Benny Jones	IRA comrade of Mac Ireland
Bobbie Johnson	Sammy Johnson's cousin
Brian Kelly	Top Special Branch man
Cassidy Brothers	(Jack and Peter) New York cops
Charlie Shepherd	SAS assassin
Chris Gaffney	Quartermaster of Belfast IRA
Eamon Mc Nally	2nd in command of Fermanagh-Cavan IRA
Emily Richardson	American reporter
Emmet Mulligan	Top Irish Republican leader
Fr. Maguire	Assassinated at altar
Harry Brogan	Chief of staff of IRA
Hugh Mc Caffery	New York cop
Jimmy Mc Govern Murray	Replacement for Packie
Kevin O'Neill	Second in command to Mac Ireland
Liam O'Neill	Kevin's replacement

Lizzie Duffy	Great-Aunt of Mick Duffy
Mary Mc Donough	Mac Ireland's wife
Michael Flynn	Special Branch man
Mick Duffy	Special Branch man
Mickey Mc Cormack	Contact man for Mac Ireland
Packie Murray	Mac Ireland's aide-de-camp
Patrick Mac Ireland	Legendary IRA Hero
Peadar Sheridan	Mac Ireland's driver
Robert Moore	SAS assassin
Roger Brady	Patriotic helper
Sammy Johnson	Protestant detective
Seamus O'Reilly	Trusted messenger
Sean O'Connell	Chief of Staff of IRA
Fr. Terence Murphy	Priest in Washington D.C.
Terence Mac Ireland	Mac Ireland's brother assassinated by British
Vera Johnson	Sammy Johnson's aunt
Vincent Fratelli	IRA Internal Security

EPIGRAPH

"Yea, from the table of my memory

I'll wipe away all trivial fond records,

All saws of books, all forms, all pressures past,

That youth and observation copied there;

And thy commandment all alone shall live

Within the book and volume of my brain,

Unmixt with baser matter; yes, by heaven!"

Hamlet. Act 1. Scene V. 98-104

CHAPTER 1

The priest reverently genuflected at the end of Mass, and the two altar boys, one on either side of him, did the same in perfect unison. The congregation belted out Faith of Our Fathers as they always did after Sunday Mass in St. Brigid's church in Kincally parish, County Fermanagh, Northern Ireland.

The parish was near to the British-imposed Border. And not only near – actually divided in two by the Border. One half was in Northern Ireland, the other half in County Cavan, in the Free State/ Irish Republic.

The moment the priest entered the sacristy to the left of the altar, he told one of the Altar Boys to go outside the Church get Seamus Reilly to come in. "Seamus Reilly the football player, Father?" the boy asked. "No, Seamus Reilly the astronaut," joked the priest. The two altar boys laughed and ran to get Seamus.

Fr. Fergal Maguire heard the heavy latch on the sacristy door being opened, and he knew it would be Seamus. "Hi ya, Father. Isn't it a lovely summer's day?" sang out the big, rangy, rawboned fellow as he bounded in. It was August 1978. Fr. Maguire was wiping clean the little hand-held black board that he used for writing instructions for the sacristan and the altar boys.

Seamus stood waiting, his big hands by his side with his thumbs stuck in his trouser pockets. His hands were so big they could never fit into any pocket. This made him a bit self-conscious – but it also made him effective on the Gaelic football field, and absolutely deadly in a fistfight. Seamus tried to avoid fights, yet if forced, his big hands would knock the daylights out of anyone who pushed him too far.

"Seamus, I wonder if you could do something really important for me."

"Sure I will, Father, anything at all."

The priest went to the door and closed it. "Seamus, I am going to write a message on this blackboard. You are to pass the message on to someone. Then I am going to wipe it out and you must never repeat it to anyone else. Do I have your word on this?"

Seamus nodded.

Fr. Maguire whispered, "You know how to get in touch with Patrick Mac Ireland?"

Seamus's amiable smile disappeared – not because he didn't trust Fr. Maguire, but because he now realized this was something really serious.

Mac Ireland was a legendary IRA leader from the parish who had been on the run for seven years. The British Army and police wanted him dead or alive. He had left his home in 1971, and had gone across the Border into the Free State, as the locals called it, but whose official title (however questionable) was the Republic of Ireland. The British had partitioned the country by the 1920 Government of Ireland Act, creating the worst possible outcome, and sowing the seeds of inevitable future conflict. The Catholics in the remaining Six

Counties of the new artificial, gerrymandered State of Northern Ireland were abandoned to the tender mercies of the Stormont Government that was dedicated to the maintenance of Protestant and Orange supremacy. The British Government could not care less how the Stormont Government treated the minority Catholics as long as the Six Counties were held for His Majesty's Government.

"Now Seamus," continued the priest as he held a small blank blackboard in his left hand. "Here's what you tell Patrick," as he wrote with a chalk-stub on the blackboard: "It is the 'Middle Name.'" Seamus read it not knowing what it referred to.

"Have you got that?" asked the priest.

"Yes, Father," whispered Seamus.

"Now repeat it silently to yourself three times before I erase it."

Seamus nodded and did what he was told.

"You must never tell anyone about this," emphasized Fr. Maguire. "NEVER! Do you understand this?"

"Yes, Father." Seamus replied. Then he headed off.

Fr. Maguire closed the outside door, and went back into the church and knelt at the altar steps, with his back to the door leading to the sacristy. He began his "thanksgiving after Mass" – a time of silent prayer in thanksgiving for the inestimable gift of the Eucharist. There he would kneel for fifteen minutes in silent prayer and meditation.

After 15 minutes, and just as he was ending his private prayers, Fr. Maguire heard the heavy latch to the outside door being lifted. That can hardly be Seamus back so soon, he thought.

As he blessed himself, he heard the footsteps behind him. Suddenly, he felt metal being pressed to the back of his head. But the good priest never heard the muffled shot that killed him instantly.

Meanwhile, Seamus had already seen Mac Ireland, gave him the message, and was on his way back.

He had been excited to meet the legendary IRA leader, and was bursting to tell his friends, yet, knew he never could. Mac Ireland had received him nicely and made him feel at home in the safe-house in which they met.

Mac Ireland had flaming red hair and a movie star smile. He looked more like a doctor or a schoolteacher, and not at all like the horrible "terrorist" the Brits tried to make him out to be.

"Bad cess to the Brits, they've always smeared and caricatured our patriots and the bloody, cowardly media goes along with it," he muttered to himself. He really wanted to use the F-word but felt "bad cess" was more proper so soon after Mass.

Seamus was soon parking his motorbike outside St. Brigid's Church. He knew Fr. Maguire would still be there praying, reading his Office or just making sure everything was in order.

Seamus opened the outside door to the sacristy, lifted the heavy latch that had survived unchanged for God knows how many years. He turned left, walked about ten feet and opened the door that led to the altar. He knew not to shout out the priest's name – reverence inside the church was long tradition in St. Brigid's.

"Oh, Christ," Seamus yelled, and instantly felt bad he had sworn. "Oh, Jesus, I shouldn't be swearing inside the church and the priest dead on the altar steps."

Fr. Maguire was lying face down at the side of the altar, half his head missing with blood splattered down the altar steps.

Once he got control of himself, Seamus bizarrely found himself thinking in really slow motion: "For centuries in this parish, when a lay-person died, the first thing you did was to send for the priest. But why don't you send for the priest when a priest has died? Who do you send for?" His next reaction was to run to the police barracks, which he knew was ridiculous because no Catholic in the parish ever trusted the police.

Finally, it occurred to him to fetch the doctor, a local Catholic who lived close by.

The doctor, immediately knowing the priest was dead, told one of the crowd that had started to gather to go and tell the police in the local barracks, about three minutes' walk from the church. Soon the police – the hated RUC (Royal Ulster Constabulary) were all over the place.

"Look at them bastards," seethed one of the bystanders. "And them probably involved in the assassination."

The police asked Seamus a few half-hearted questions and then dismissed him.

Seamus knew what he had to do. He jumped on his motorbike, made sure the police were not following him, and roared off across The Border to find Mac Ireland again.

Mac Ireland had moved base since Seamus had met him, but some of the IRA security people knew where he was, and brought Seamus to him.

When Mac Ireland heard what happened, he was devastated and seemed to shrink to half his size. To avoid crying, he relied on an old trick he had learned: he cupped his left hand over his mouth, with his thumb extended at the side of his head, and pressed upwards under his nose. This not only made it easier to breathe, it also, for some reason he did not understand, helped to hold back the tears. He had known Fr. Maguire for many years and had total respect for him as a priest and as an Irishman. He thanked Seamus, and quickly sent him off so that he could grieve in private. It was Fr. Maguire's message to me that got him killed: 'it's the Middle Name.' Instantly he knew what he had to do – get the person who assassinated Fr. Maguire, and bring him to justice. And since he could not bring the killer before a regular court, he would have to bring him to the ultimate court of justice.

However, Mac Ireland also knew he wouldn't be able to do anything at all if he didn't quickly move base as he now could be caught, and shot on sight. He called in his men, "Let's go, boys. Our security may have been breached." And they quickly disappeared into the nearby mountains.

There was a huge turnout for Fr. Maguire's funeral. Mac Ireland was not surprised to hear that the local Bishop stayed away.

He thought to himself: "The Bishop was scared of controversy as Fr. Maguire was seen as too militant on The Troubles. The only way to get to be Bishop in Ireland was to keep your mouth shut about The Troubles. Never severely criticize the Brits, and never condemn the weak-kneed Dublin Government. And then the Bishops had the bloody cheek to lecture people about not resorting to violence to resist oppression. One can only preach nonviolence by first practicing non-violence, like Gandhi and Martin Luther King, Jr. did. They not only talked the talk, but walked the walk, and, therefore, had moral authority. If one does not nonviolently resist oppression, one has no moral right to condemn those who resort to armed struggle. If people who have moral power don't use it to nonviolently resist, the poor and powerless will eventually take up arms. And the Bishops have no moral right to condemn them."

The British army and the RUC kept a respectful distance from the grave as Fr. Maguire was lowered into the ground. However, a helicopter hovered overhead photographing the crowd, which was their common surveillance practice.

Fr. Maguire was – before the assassin's bullet stole his life – 48-years old, a short stocky Cavan man with jet-black hair. He had the face of movie cowboy – lined and battered by the elements – even though he was more of a sheep man. When he wasn't looking after his parish, he was tending his sheep on the side. That was his idea of time off.

People were surprised to learn that as a young man he was a sub on the Cavan football team at a time when Cavan still knew how to kick football – 1947-1952. He would regale his friends with stories of the Cavan greats: John Joe O'Reilly, PJ. Duke, and The Gunner Brady.

The priest hid his brilliant mind under, I'm just a "simple-farmer-act." Had he not been a priest, people might have classed him as "a cute Cavan hoor" – but only in the best possible sense! (In Kincally, the word "hoor" was never used about a woman. It was a fairly mild expletive, indeed, hardly an expletive at all. Sometimes it could be used as a term of affection. It was less severe than "bastard," almost like "a bad rascal" or "crafty rogue." When combined with "cute" it meant "too clever by half." "Cute" never meant pretty or attractive, as in the

American sense.).

Fr. Maguire was loved and respected by all in Kincally. He was a rare phenomenon: a patriot-priest.

He was a man who had loved his God and his Church and who had refused to be bullied into thinking he could not also love his country. He did not buy into the fashionable ecclesiastical drivel that the more a priest was removed from and indifferent to The Troubles, the better priest he was. It drove him crazy that Irish Bishops were expressing concern about injustice all over the globe, yet ignoring British oppression in The North.

"Where's the logic in that, not to mention the theology or morality," he constantly marveled.

"How can the Irish Hierarchy cry for the oppressed people in South Africa and Latin America, and still ignore the prisoners in Long Kesh, the torture of political prisoners, the shoot-to-kill policy of Her Majesty's Government and systematic anti-Catholic discrimination? It's enough to make a man a Protestant."

On the other hand, Fr. Maguire had been encouraged by the 1977 appointment of Tomas O'Fiaich as Archbishop of Armagh to replace the late, and quite useless Cardinal Conway. He regarded Conway as being scared of the Brits, and more concerned about the "sacredness" of his own office than about the suffering of the Catholic people – a historic flaw in so many "princes of the Church." How the hell, anyway, Fr. Maguire would muse did Cardinals – allegedly followers of the homeless-persecuted-crucified Christ – ever come to be considered princes. Nothing could be farther removed from the image of Christ than a prince (except, of course, a Queen or King).

Fr. Maguire, feared, however, that no matter how good

O'Fiaich might be, the other Bishops would box him in and marginalize him. Indeed, the ferret-faced Cathal Daly of Ardagh and Clanmacnoise was already calling O'Fiach, behind his back, "Provo Tom." The Irish Establishment and the compliant press were constantly promoting Daly as a great intellectual and theologian in the hope that he would overshadow what they saw as the republicanism of O'Fiaich.

Before he had been made a bishop – a position he relentlessly sought after – Daly had taught for many years in Queens University Belfast – then a bastion of anti-Catholic discrimination. Yet, the lily-livered Daly never opened his mouth. His "position," not truth or justice, was all that mattered.

A Church that would be controlled by such Bishops would surely come to harm, Fr. Maguire always feared.

Why were the Bishops so scared of the Brits? he constantly tried to figure out.

And how could Bishops get away with covering up the teaching of the Catholic Church on justice? Admittedly, the Catholic Church was late in the game talking about social justice. The first Papal encyclical, Rerum Novarum, wasn't published until 1891 – almost half a century after The Communist Manifesto.

However, the Church had since been trying to catch up, even though the Irish Bishops didn't seem to be aware of it. For example, Pope John XXIII had published his important encyclical Pacem in Terris in 1963 – declaring peace to be like a house built on four pillars: truth, justice, love and freedom. Couldn't the Bishops see that the House of Northern Ireland was not built on those four pillars? Their only notion of peace was that the IRA would quit fighting and that Catholics should be content to stay "at the back of the bus."

Then the Second Vatican Council's document "Gaudium et Spes," and later Pope Paul VI's encyclical "Populorum Progresso" (1967) gave fresh perspective to Church social teaching.

And then on November 30, 1971, the Bishops Synod meeting in Rome issued "Justice in the World," roundly and prophetically (if somewhat late): "... Action on behalf of justice and participation in the transformation of the world fully appear to us as a constitutive dimension of the preaching of the Gospel."

The Irish Bishops must have missed that Synod, Fr. Maguire used to quip. All across Ireland, North and South, the Bishops had a conspiracy of silence to cover-up church teaching lest, if they taught it to the natives, it might give aid and comfort to the IRA. That was the Bishops' eleventh commandment – that superseded all others – "Thou shall not say anything about British injustice lest it help the IRA and annoy the Brits." It was also the golden rule of the Dublin government.

"No wonder poor Ireland is such a 'distressful country,'" Fr. Maguire would often lament: "The Bishops are scared of their own teaching, and the Dublin Government is scared of their own Constitution." ... Indeed, that may have been his very last thought on this earth before the assassin's bullet sent him into eternity.

CHAPTER 2

Patrick Mac Ireland was a member of a large family – five brothers and four sisters.

His older brother, and the eldest of the family, Terence, was killed during the IRA Border Campaign, codenamed Operation Harvest (December 1956 - February 1962).

Terence had been on the run for five years and was sneaking across the fields to visit his parents at Christmas, 1961.

An undercover unit of British Special Forces lay in ambush. They shot him down like a dog, even though he was unarmed, with his hands high above his head.

The Brits assassinated Terence to intimidate and terrorize the Mac Ireland family into submission – the classic mistake of the British throughout Irish history.

Patrick, then 17, instead of being intimidated joined the IRA on New Year's Day, January I, 1962. And he did so even though the IRA commander for the overall South Fermanagh-Cavan area confided to him that the IRA campaign was about to be called off. And, indeed it was, on February 26.

However, Mac Ireland knew the IRA would rise again – "like the Phoenix from the ashes" – and he planned to be fully ready when that day came. For the next ten years, he read voraciously – history, philosophy, sociology, politics, economics, and religion. He devoured literature on revolutionary theory and the art of war. And he began to secretly build a series of well-hidden dugouts across the Border in county Cavan. ... All the while, as he kept the small, poor family farm going.

Patrick, nonetheless, was never just a "militarist" – believing in physical force just for the sake of it.

When the Civil Rights Campaign began in 1968, he played his full part – he protested, marched, did "sit-ins" – all non-violently.

But when Unionist/Protestant mobs – encouraged and enabled by the RUC and B Specials – burned down Bombay Street, the Catholic street in Belfast, in August 1969, Mac Ireland knew it was just a matter of time before he would go on the run. On February 6, 1971, the Belfast IRA shot the first British soldier in the new phase of the Troubles.

That was the signal for Mac Ireland to go on the run. He had crossed the Cavan border, and had not returned to his home since then. He would not make the same mistake as big brother, Terence. And he had pledged he would never be shot with his hands up. He would only go down fighting. He would never surrender to the Brits.

Now in 1978, Mac Ireland was 34. He had grown into a strikingly handsome man, which was surprising because while he was still at home, he wasn't considered as handsome as his other brothers. That was because he had been worn out with the strain of being, in effect, the head of the family as his father was old, keeping the farm going by day and training as a soldier by night. It was a backbreaking existence, and it left him looking drained and haggard.

It was, therefore, most ironic to the family that Patrick actually gained weight, and started looking much better after he had gone on the run... Ironic, but delightful. His thin, wiry frame bulked up, and his face filled out.

After seven years on the run, Mac Ireland was – every inch of his six-foot frame – very much the leading man, as they say in Hollywood

At nighttime Patrick went to visit his wife at another safe house. Nobody knew he was married except Fr. Maguire who had secretly performed the wedding five years after he went on the run. It was just too dangerous for people to know they were married.

His wife, Mary McDonough, a 26-year-old Cavan girl, was a tall slim brunette with blue eyes. She taught French and Irish in the Secondary School in Cavan town. Mary, an ardent Irish Republican was widely admired for her intelligence, beauty and independence. She had been offered several university positions and had turned them down, reluctant to give up her country life for Dublin's city life. Furthermore, she didn't need the money as her grandparents had left her independently wealthy. Now she was glad she had not relocated to Dublin, as she would never have met Mac Ireland. She had first met him when he attended the evening Irish class she taught in Belturbet for adults who wanted to be more proficient in Gaelic. His red hair, radiant smile and respectful manner immediately caught her Cavan eye. Indeed, she was the one who asked him out, Fermanagh folk being a little bit more reserved. He leveled with her immediately that because of his commitment to the

Irish Cause, a normal relationship would be extremely difficult – that, indeed, she could be a widow at an early age. None of that could change Mary's heart. This was the guy for her, and they had to make the best of the tumultuous times they were living in. "If it's true love – love that knows no fear – how can we let danger stop us?" she had asked him. Mac Ireland could not dispute that, nor did he want to.

When Mac Ireland broke the news of Fr. Maguire's death to Mary, she completely broke down, as she respected the priest as much as Mac Ireland did. Fr. Maguire used to visit them every few months. He would celebrate Mass for just the two of them as the IRA men kept watch – "Just as in the Penal Law days," Fr. Maguire exclaimed.

"Who could have killed him, Patrick?" Mary sobbed.

"The SAS or some such other British special forces," he explained.

He did not mention the message that Fr. Maguire had sent through Seamus Reilly.

Then Mary caught hold of him and pleaded, "You must be really, really careful. You are in enough danger without reacting foolishly to Father's assassination."

He nodded, held her tight, and assured her he would not take any risks, but knowing that that is exactly what he would have to do. There was no way he could not. "Don't worry, Mary. I'll be careful. Now I have to run."

And with that he was off into the night.

"It's the Middle Name," Fr. Maguire's message kept repeating itself in Mac Ireland's head. Did it mean that the Brits know Fr. Maguire had sent the message? Not necessarily. He was certain Seamus Reilly had not divulged it. Maybe the killer just knew that Fr. Maguire was onto him.

Mac Ireland got out of the car, bid good-bye to the two IRA lads who had driven him through the darkness. Then he took to the mountains, to one of the dugouts he had systematically constructed all across the mountains bordering Northern Ireland. This night he would go to one of his favorites. It was tucked into the side of the mountain almost underground and totally invisible. It had a small bed, lots of books, enough food for a month and enough guns to give the Brits a fight should they cross The Border to snatch him. He had told his mother that he would never be taken alive. His family and those who knew him well were in no doubt that he would never surrender.

He knelt by the little bed and recited his night prayers, the five mysteries of the Rosary – something he had never missed doing in his entire life. Some of the young IRA men used to laugh at his spiritual side; never to his face, however, as they respected him too much. As he lay down, he thought how nice it would be if Mary could stay with him some night in his little dugout, but he knew it was just too dangerous. God rest Fr. Maguire, he prayed, as he turned over on his left side and sent straight to sleep.

The following morning, Mac Ireland was wakened by the tapping of a metal disk that was placed on a metal plate in the corner of the dugout. It was a pre-arranged signal for emergency use only. A clever, but simple device. The metal disk was attached to fishing line that ran for about three hundred yards through the back wall of the dugout through the side of the mountain, ending up in a well-concealed rock formation.

Just a few IRA men knew where the "doorbell" was located. All they had to do was pull the fishing line three times to alert Patrick. He quickly opened the strong, heavily disguised metal door, letting in a short, sturdy man in his 30s. "Come quickly, Patrick, the Brits appear to be crossing the Border over the mountain. There are 15 heavily armed soldiers and we heard a helicopter in the vicinity."

By now Mac Ireland was fully dressed. He strapped on his gun and grabbed his ammunition.

"Get the grenades, Packie," he commanded. "How many of our men are ready?"

"Seven," replied Packie.

"Do they have the Shoulder to Air Missile?

"Yes," Packie responded.

Both men moved quickly.

Patrick was 36, about 5'11" with a strong wiry build. While not an athlete, he was in great shape. Once he went on the run, he had given up drinking and smoking. He could trek over the mountains all day and night, and still be ready to take on the Brits in a firefight. He was known for his practice of taking off his boots, hanging them around his neck, when he was crossing rivers. On one occasion, he spent all night standing up to his neck in bog-hole water, as he hid from a British Army search party.

"Okay, Packie, keep up now. We're going to have to go at a bit of a gallop."

"No problem, Patrick, replied Packie Murray. The two had known each other all their lives.

Within a half an hour, they had traveled across the

side of the mountain in the Free State (Irish Republic). They linked up with the other seven IRA men, all of whom smartly saluted Mac Ireland as the leader of the Flying Column for the entire border area between Cavan and South Fermanagh. There were other IRA leaders who may have had more authority, yet everyone knew that the undisputed leader – the man in charge – in that area was Mac Ireland. Part of the secret of his success as a leader was that he never asked his men/women to do anything that he was not prepared to do himself. When other IRA leaders would tell him that he took too many risks, he always replied: "If you are not prepared to take risks, you forfeit the moral right to lead."

Mac Ireland took the binoculars from his second in command, Kevin O'Neill, and peered down the mountain – really a large hill, heavily over-grown with heather, rushes and bushes.

He could spot the Brits – a deadly team of highly trained soldiers.

No matter how much he detested England's rule in his part of Ireland (the North, the Six Counties, Northern Ireland), he nevertheless recognized that they were probably the best-trained counter-insurgency army in the world. "And why wouldn't they be," he would flash his famous smile. "Sure their entire history has been one of trying to crush insurgencies around the world to maintain the British Empire."

Now fifteen deadly representatives of that dying Empire were fast approaching.

"They are heading for the crossing we anticipated," Mac Ireland instructed as he watched through the binoculars. "Our mines were placed the other night in exactly the right spot."

Then he commanded, "The moment after Benny sets off the explosion we open up and give the survivors everything we've got. If they try to run for it, Packie, use that powerful right arm of yours to hurl the grenades. And now, boys, take deep breaths, stay calm and fight like Irishmen."

The moment the British soldiers started throwing their legs across a long barbed wire fence – the only access in an area surrounded by steep rocks on either side – Benny Jones set off the charge by remote control. A powerful explosion rocked the mountainside. The earth around the British soldiers erupted like a small volcano – stones, fence posts, shrubs, all caught up in the deadly outpouring. And in the middle of the debris, yards up in the air, the mangled bodies of British soldiers – never to touch the earth alive again.

"Now, boys," commanded Mac Ireland, "get the other six."

The IRA column opened up with a fusillade of withering fire.

Three British soldiers went down immediately. The other three tried to make a run for it toward the only way out. Packie, however, had manned that position. From behind a steep ditch, he let fly with ferocious rapidity. The grenades exploded with a thunderous bang – not as loud, of course, as the mine explosion yet still with deadly effect. Two of the soldiers were killed instantly. The remaining one, although injured, opened up and blazed away at the ditch that was providing perfect protection to Packie.

"Stop him from getting closer to Packie," ordered

Mac Ireland. With that, the entire column mowed down the last soldier. "May his soul go straight to heaven, and damn the Government that sent him to our country," declared Mac Ireland, intoning his famous mantra every time the IRA killed a British soldier.

He gathered his men around him: "Now steady up boys. It's always shaky after a fight like this. We've got to move, and move quickly because the helicopter will soon be upon us. Head for the clump of trees. I will try to draw their fire and lead them to the trees. The moment the helicopter is within firing range, use the missile and bring it down. Don't worry about me. Concentrate on the helicopter. I know this mountain like the back of my hand. I know where to shelter."

The column took off and within minutes was hidden among the trees. As if on cue, the feared Lynx helicopter arrived with its sophisticated surveillance technology, the pilot, the officer in charge, and the guy with the deadly firepower – the gunner.

Mac Ireland opened up with his AK-47 assault rifle, aware he wouldn't hit the helicopter – just wanting to get its attention. The he started to run down a side of the mountain in his famous zig zag pattern.

Years earlier, before he went on the run, one of his younger brothers – as both of them were coming down the mountain after visiting relatives in the area – was surprised by Mac Ireland's running pattern. He would later realize it was a guerilla military maneuver – don't run straight down the mountain as the young brother was doing, rather zig zag.

By now the helicopter had spotted Mac Ireland, and the machine gunner was raking the mountainside with devastating fire. He knew he only had split seconds to pull off his plan. He stopped and quite brazenly returned fire. Then he plunged into a thicket of shrubs, heather, and nettles. For all his hardiness, he hated nettles. "The damned nettles give me blisters as big as hen eggs," he would complain. However, nettles and all, he knew this thicket would keep him safe. It led, underneath all the growth, to a virtual "reversed cave" ten feet beneath solid rock. The only entrance was a two-foot hole at the base of a large oak tree, facing the outcropping of a huge rock formation just a few yards away. Instead of going under the huge rock, the cave went away from it, ten feet underground. That's why Mac Ireland always considered it a "reversed cave." The helicopter could not fire upon the cave without crashing into a higher section of the mountain.

Mac Ireland scrambled through the hole, grabbed the rope ladder that he had placed there for such occasions, and descended into the safety of the cool, rock-solid cave.

The helicopter fired what appeared like endless rounds, but Mac Ireland knew he was in no danger unless, of course, the helicopter unleashed its TOW missiles, which were capable of taking out half the mountainside. That was unlikely because the Brits had never used those missiles in The North. Thus, he felt he was in no real danger – the helicopter was.

To get the proper firing position on the thicket, the helicopter had to repeatedly make runs that brought it nearer to the IRA column that was hiding in the clump of trees with the shoulder-to-air missile. He didn't know too much about firing the missile; however, he made sure Kevin O'Neill had become expert in the field (no pun intended).

"All right Kevin," he whispered to himself, "blow the hoors from the Irish skies." And for the second time within a half hour, the helicopter performed as if on cue – placing itself in perfect position for Kevin's on-coming missile.

It was over in seconds. The deadly machine gun fire ceased the intimidating whirling of the helicopter stopped – to be replaced by a blinding fireball in the sky amid circling smoke and carnage.

Mac Ireland climbed out of "reversed cave" and headed for the rest of the Column.

"There's no need to check, Patrick. They are all dead. No one could survive that fireball," stated Kevin.

Mac Ireland nodded, adding, "Just as well, we have no time. The Free State Army and the Guards will be all over the place. Not to challenge the Brits for violating Free State national sovereignty, but to arrest us."

"Or shoot us," seethed Kevin.

The shameful way the Free State collaborated with the Brits was a constant source of Republican anger and fury.

Patrick then gathered them closer, put his hands on the shoulders of the two lads standing closest to him: "You have performed well, boys. You have fought bravely. Now break up, go your separate ways, and we meet tonight in the safe house which Packie will later reveal to you. Kevin, if you need me in the meantime, send Packie for me. "Good luck, boys, and with that he was off at a steady run.

As the Column watched him go, one remarked, "We

have one of the best leaders Ireland has ever produced."

"Why do you think his second name is Mac Ireland?" Kevin quipped. The others smiled.

"Of such, legends are made," whispered Kevin softly as he watched Mac Ireland disappear from view.

CHAPTER 3

Mac Ireland walked through the door of the pre-arranged safe house at 8 PM.

He was pleased to see all the eight men present. Despite his famous steely self-control, one thing drove him crazy – people being routinely late. It made him really lose his composure. It was unacceptable and offensive any time, but it was particularly unacceptable for a guerilla movement. It could get his men killed or arrested.

"Good men, you're all on time," Mac Ireland said.

When asked, each of the eight men present told him they were fine. They had eaten and slept and had recovered from that ferocious battle with the British Army.

"Kevin, you chair the meeting and go over the stuff we need to deal with, and I will add a few things when we've finished," he directed.

Kevin had been a medical student at a Dublin University and had quit to go full time with the IRA. He was bright, cool under fire and loyal to his men. Mac Ireland was well pleased with him as his second-in-command. Kevin was from Tyrone – a hardy county that produced formidable IRA men and women.

Although he was from Tyrone and would have normally joined his local unit in that County, O'Neill wanted to serve under Mac Ireland. Well that ... and because he was dating a Cavan girl, also medical student.

Kevin was a born leader. People just automatically deferred to him. He was continually told that he looked like a young Sean Connery – dark and handsome, suave and charming but with, when needed, a hint of menace. A totally dependable man.

He was 28 years old and 5' 11." Very well built – 190 pounds, not an ounce of fat. Very large powerful hands, an iron man, in body and mind. Nothing would stop this Tyrone man, except victory or death. Mac Ireland loved him like a brother and trusted him with his life.

Kevin began to speak in his measured and precise manner.

"The latest intelligence we have on the State execution of Fr. Maguire is that he was assassinated by a well-dressed man in smart casuals. Our eyewitness is a Protestant woman from Kincally parish. As is her custom, she waited until all the Sunday Mass traffic had left from around St. Brigid's. As she cycled toward the church, she saw a man quickly leave the church, vault over the 4ft. wall, 'as if it were only six inches high,' the woman claimed. Then he dashed like an Olympic athlete to an unmarked car parked five hundred yards down the road facing the Cuilcagh Mountains, which Patrick knows well."

Kevin paused, looked around the table and was taken aback to observe Mac Ireland's face transfixed with grief. He tried not to stare and kept talking: "There's no great mystery with what we are dealing with here.

This was no fanatical Protestant Orangeman shooting a priest. It has all the hallmarks of the SAS or one of the other British Special Operations."

Then he stopped, looked at Mac Ireland, "Patrick, do you want to take it from here."

Mac Ireland cleared his throat and prayed he could speak in a steady voice.

"I am from Kincally parish. Not only was Fr. Maguire a close and trusted friend, was he also a great Irishman. I am familiar with every person in the parish. Therefore, I will be assuming direct and complete responsibility for this case. You men have enough to do. Kevin will be in charge until I assume control again, and Packie will be number two. Keep the flying column flying, boys. Do not let up. Hit the Brits as hard as you can. For the time being, do not bring in any new recruits for I fear there is great danger of us being penetrated by Brit or Free State intelligence. And, as I have always warned you, do not go drinking in the local villages, which are crawling with agents and informers. The Brits are spreading around a lot of money."

Then he jumped up from the table, went to a cupboard, turned around, flashed his famous smile: "And talking about drink, let me stand all of you one or two, for you performed like real Irish patriots today."

And with that, he pulled from the cupboard a huge bottle of Powers whiskey. "I don't touch it myself, but tonight you men deserve a treat!"

"Ah, thanks be to Jaysus," chortled Packie.

They clinked their glasses, wished each other health and uttered in unison, "Up the Republic," referring, of course, not to the partitioned 26-County Free State but to the real 32-County Republic declared by the heroes of Easter Week, 1916. That was the only Republic these men gave their allegiance to. It was the Republic (a United, Independent Ireland) to which they had dedicated their young lives, and for which they were prepared to die – like so many before them.

By their second glass of Powers, the men were visibly beginning to relax. None of them drank much, and hadn't touched a drop for weeks, so the two drinks were starting a buzz on each of them.

One of the youngest lads Eamon Mc Nally, only 18, asked, "Patrick, what do you think of all this chat about a possible truce between the Brits and the IRA?"

"Well Eamon," responded Mac Ireland, "we all realize that someday there will be talks. All wars end in talks. And as that old hoor, Churchill, declared back in 1954 at The White House 'to jaw-jaw is better than to war-war.' I am as political as the next man. I understand there has to be a political solution, and even a compromise because nobody gets one hundred per cent of everything. I just hope that when a compromise is reached, it is an honorable one, and a transparent one. That it is not just another British solution, dressed up as a genuine sharing of power by all the people on the island of Ireland. After all the sacrifices, I hope we are not tricked again by the Brits, leaving it to our grandchildren to pick up the pieces. However, equally, I believe that when The Movement reaches an agreement with the British, then it is our obligation to honor that agreement. We must stick together, and we must not split."

Packie then noticed the book Mac Ireland had brought with him, as was his habit, for he was rarely without a book. "What's your current reading, Patrick?"

"It's about Palestine – the other Holy Land partitioned by England," laughed Mac Ireland.

"Would you tell the lads a bit about the history of Palestine," Packie asked.

Mac Ireland willingly obliged, as it was one of his favorite subjects.

He began: "Lads, no Irishman can fail to sympathize with the Palestinians. I am also deeply sympathetic to the historic worldwide mistreatment of the Jews. And to my great shame, the Catholic Church also contributed to this mistreatment – as did the Protestant churches. And, of course, The Holocaust has covered us all in shame and guilt, making it difficult for us to speak openly and honestly about the mistreatment of the Palestinians.

And the same bastards – Lloyd George and Churchill – who carved up Palestine did the same to Ireland – purely in England's imperial interest.

Lloyd George predicted that history would remember Lord Balfour, 'like the scent on a pocket-handkerchief.'

But, putdown aside, he was quite wrong because Balfour is forever remembered in Irish history as "Bloody Balfour" and because he gave his name to the Brit statement that would initiate the partition of Palestine – the Balfour Declaration, 1917."

"Oh my God," said Packie, "was Lord Balfour the same as Bloody Balfour?"

"Aye, Packie, the same hoor," replied Mac Ireland. "He was nicknamed Bloody Balfour for his cruelty as Chief Secretary for Ireland in 1887-1891 – during the Irish Land War.

So England, in effect, partitioned Palestine in 1917

(the UN rubber-stamping it in 1947) and partitioned Ireland by the 1920 Government of Ireland Act.

England couldn't wait to get its dirty hands on Palestine. Even Prime Minister Asquith would record that his Cabinet were like a 'gang of buccaneers' when they discussed Palestine. Furthermore, he would claim that Lloyd George, 'does not care a damn for the Jews or their past or their future.' England, in fact, wanted a client (the Jews) in the Middle East – as an excuse for intervening in the affairs of the Ottoman Empire.

However, there was also a semi-religious dimension to this: it harked back to the Puritan distorted interpretation of Scripture that the Messiah would come once the Jews were returned to their ancestral land. So English imperialists could always exploit this when needed. But as you lads know, England's colonialism always trumped England's Protestantism.

I should add here that the Balfour Declaration had also this two-fold objective: to encourage American Zionists to maneuver the Untied States into entering the First World War (which, by the way, was as much about saving Britain's empire as anything else) and to detach Russian Jews from Bolshevism."

Mac Ireland paused, and added: "The United States is also to blame. President Woodrow Wilson (1913-1921), for all his grand talk about national self-determination, never opposed the partition of Palestine or Ireland. Even though one of his advisors warned that the Brits were making the Middle East a "breeding place for future war." Of course, President Wilson was a segregationist, and a self-described Orangeman. Anyway, the end result was that although the Palestinians had lived in that land for over a thousand years, and owned over 90 per cent of the land, it was stolen from right underneath them. On November 29, 1947, the UN, shamelessly acting as England's poodle, gave 56 per cent of Palestine to the Zionists, who would go on to declare independence in 1948 and define Israel a "Jewish state." Simultaneously, they had made plans to take over the entire Palestinian land mass by expelling the Palestinians by any means necessary. By 1949, Israel had conquered 78 per cent of Palestine, violently expelling three-quarter of a million Palestinians. These Palestinian refugees are still at the heart of the Israeli-Palestinian conflict. Palestinians refer to this ethnic cleansing as The Nakba (The Disaster). And they do so in the same tone as the Irish refer to The Famine, and almost with a shiver, in hushed voices. After the 1967 War (Six Days War), Israel occupied the remaining 22 per cent of Palestine. Ah, poor Palestine and poor Ireland. We were pawns in England's dirty little game."

Finally, Mac Ireland stopped, sighed deeply and said, "Now lads you've got me on my hobby horse, and I have to get off."

But young Mc Nally, now lit up by the warmth of the whiskey, and honored to get the chance to chat with Mac Ireland, suddenly intercepted and changed the subject.

"Patrick, some of the younger volunteers, especially the city lads and lassies say you are too religious."

Mac Ireland threw his head back and laughed heartedly. Kevin was pleased to see that – it was taking Mac Ireland's mind off Fr. Maguire's assassination for a moment – like what happens at an Irish wake when the gathered neighbors chat about everything under the sun – religion, politics, football, the weather, etc., etc. – bringing relief and catharsis.

Mac Ireland continued: "Eamon, have you or any of the men, or lassies, as you call them, ever seen me trying to impose my religious views on anyone? I do not wear my religion on my sleeve. I only discuss it with those who genuinely inquire about it."

Eamon impishly retorted, "Would you allow me to 'genuinely inquire,' Patrick?"

"Of course, I would as long as we are not imposing our conversation on the others."

"No, not at all," interjected Kevin. "It will be a break from politics and The Cause."

The others eagerly assented and pulled their chairs closer.

"So, then what are your religious views, Patrick?" asked Eamon – fairly relishing that he was being listened to and taken seriously.

"Well," smiled Patrick," I am not an Anglican or Calvinist. And, I'm not a member of Paisley's church."

That got a laugh from them all.

"I am a convinced, practicing Catholic. I don't pretend to be a perfect Catholic – far from it. Still, I do firmly believe in the Catholic Church. Historically and theologically, I consider it to be the Church that has preserved completely both the Old Testament and the New Testament, and has faithfully handed down the teachings of Jesus Christ. I cannot belong to a church that only stretches back in history twenty years or a hundred years, 500 years or even 1000 years. I have to belong to a Church that goes all the way back to the New Testament. Whatever Christ intended, surely one cannot believe His intention was to found hundreds of thousands of different denominations, each claiming to be the one true Church of Christ? Surely that cannot be the case? And surely when Christ promised The Holy Spirit would be with the Church until the end of time, surely He had to mean it? I respect all the other Churches but I feel that in certain aspects they lack the fullness of Christ's revelation – that they broke with Apostolic tradition at the Reformation. However, I am pleased to see that progress has been made between the Lutherans and Anglicans regarding The Eucharist. And I think the Lutherans and the Catholic Church will one day reach agreement on Justification – the wedge issue of The Reformation. Unfortunately, Luther and the Catholic Church just shouted at each other, instead of listening. They were essentially saying the same thing. But you know when a fight starts, things escalate, and the fight becomes about all sorts of things, instead of the original point of disagreement. But just let me add this: At least with Luther, The Reformation was religious and theological. In England it was only political. Inevitably, in Ireland, too, it was about politics. The horrible anti-Catholicism that was developed was not about The Reformation, rather it was simply another arrow in Britain's quiver for keeping the Catholics down. Sadly, the Protestants were recruited into that oppressive system. Many of them thought they were standing up for The Reformation when, in fact, they were simply being used to keep the Catholics down. It had nothing to do with Transubstantiation, only with England's power."

Then Mac Ireland stopped and laughed. He looked around his men, and asked: "Would any of you be familiar with the famous blind Irish poet, Raftery, who lived in the late 1700s?" None of them had, so Mac Ireland continued, "The reason I was laughing is that I was reminded of one of Raftery's verses that I hadn't thought of for a long time:

> *Don't talk of your Protestant Minister*
> *Or his church without Temple or state*
> *For the foundation stone of his religion*
> *Was the bollocks of Henry VIII."*

The men thought it was hilarious and laughed loudly; and, Kevin said, "Repeat it again, Patrick." And he did.

Eamon couldn't wait to jump in, "But look at all the bad things the Catholic Church did throughout the centuries."

"And the Church will continue to do bad things, Eamon, because it is made up of people like you and me. I'm not sure if you consider yourself a Catholic. But for as long as the Church is made up of sinners, there will be sin. Christ did not say we would be sinless but that with His grace we can struggle to overcome sin. An institution that has been around for two thousand years is bound to have bad things in its history. Look at the Free State government. It has only been around since 1922, and look at all the bad things it has done."

That lightened the mood and elicited a chuckle all round.

Patrick looked around at the others, "Now boys, I don't want to be seen as preaching here."

"No, no," insisted Kevin, "carry on. This can be a great conversation."

Eamon jumps in again, "But, Patrick, what does it really mean to you to be Catholic?"

"Catholic," Mac Ireland replied, "means universal." The opposite of Catholicism is not Protestantism – but sectarianism. Being a Catholic means to me that I am a member of the universal Church, not a sect or splinter group. The Church is the mystical Body of Christ – and Christ has only one body. One body, one faith, one baptism. Just as Christ is the Sacrament of God, the Church is the Sacrament of Christ in the world. Baptism not only made me a member of a group, it also baptized me into the death and resurrection of Jesus Christ. Through the Church, I become part of the Mystical Body of Christ, a member of the people of God, whose mission is to build up God's kingdom on earth – a kingdom of truth, justice, love and forgiveness, where we treat everyone, especially the poor, as if he or she were Jesus Christ Himself.

That's what being a Catholic means to me. I am the first to confess that I don't live up to it, falling short all the time. Still, I struggle on, relying on God's grace, mercy and forgiveness. Despite my failures, I deeply believe we are all the brothers and sisters of Christ. And that is particularly serious to me because today we killed eighteen brothers of Christ – the British soldiers who came to kill us."

He paused and didn't speak again for a long time. The others sat in silence, pondering the awful seriousness of what they were about as guerillas fighting for justice and freedom.

Mac Ireland then continued: "However, let's not take up the issue of violence versus non-violence. Let's just stick to the issue of membership in the Church. For me, I must belong to the Body of Christ – I need the sacraments. After all, it was through the Sacrament of Baptism that I became a member of the Body of Christ. I need to go to Mass to keep one of Christ's most important commandments: Do this in memory of me."

At this, Eamon interjected, "One of our leaders recently claimed we don't need to go to Confession – that we can cut out the middle man."

"Oh, bollocks!" shot back Mac Ireland, taking everybody by surprise as he usually didn't speak like that. "I've never known a Catholic who saw the priest as a 'middle man.' Furthermore, do you think when a priest himself goes to Confession he sees the other priest as 'the middle man'? Of course not. That's a total distortion of the Sacrament of Confession or Reconciliation, as it is called today. The priest, among other things, is a minister of the Sacraments. You might as well say cut out Baptism, cut out preaching, cut out the New Testament, cut out even Jesus Himself, and the Holy Spirit. Deal directly with God the Father."

Not wanting to be seen as "preaching," Mac Ireland then complained, "You fellas got me talking too much. Packie, you are not going to be able to reach me for some time. Good luck boys."

And with that, he was off into the night.

Kevin looked at Eamon with a huge grin, "Well, young fella, what did you think of that?"

"Jaysus, it was great. I've never heard anyone talk like that before," Eamon gushed.

"Ha," replied Kevin, "You should hear him when he really talks theology. In the early days, we were once in a Dublin hotel bar, and nobody there knew us. A group was engaged in a lively conversation about the

Church and theology. It turned out that they were a group of students and teachers from Maynooth College – the Seminary that once only had clerical students, and now has seminarians, plus all sorts of students – male and female?" The others nodded they were aware of Maynooth. "Well," continued Kevin, "somehow or other, Patrick and I got caught up in the conversation. And you should have seen the looks on the faces of the students when Patrick started quoting the documents of the Second Vatican Council, St. Thomas Aquinas, and Martin Luther. He's a well-read man with deep knowledge of history, religion, and politics. They no longer make men like Patrick Mac Ireland."

Here Kevin stopped: "Lads, this has gone on long enough. It was a grand night, and I hope we have others like it, but now we must go. We have work to do tomorrow."

CHAPTER 4

Mac Ireland was conscious he was taking an enormous risk. The night after the meeting with the eight men, he was slipping across the Border into The North, all by himself with absolutely no back up. He felt one man would attract less attention than a group. He was aware if he was going to get cooperation from the person he was going to visit, he should not come with an IRA patrol. He knew the Protestant woman who had witnessed to the assassin running from St. Brigid's. He needed to speak to her in person.

Mac Ireland moved steadily through the darkness. When he came to a shallow river, off came his boots to be hung around his neck. Wading the stream soundlessly, he kept a watchful eye for the Brits or RUC. However, he was in luck – the way was clear, and he was soon approaching the Protestant woman's farmhouse. Before reaching the door, he put his Smith and Wesson pistol in a small clump of rose bushes.

He guessed the woman would be on her own because her husband died some years back. He knocked on the kitchen window, as country folk commonly do.

The moment she saw it was Mac Ireland, she waved and hurried to the door.

"Patrick, no matter how surprised I am, you're welcome here," and she held out her strong countrywoman's hand.

"How are you, Mrs. Johnson?"

Vera Johnson was about 5'7", in her late seventies, and despite her age, was as straight as a die. She was a plain woman with the well-scrubbed look, no make-up, perhaps sometimes a little lipstick. No perfume ever. Her once brown, now mostly gray hair was swept back and neatly held in a bun with hairpins. Her round-rimmed glasses kept slipping down her nose.

The King James Bible held a place of honor in the sitting room. It was positioned on a tall antique lectern desk to the right of the mantel piece, and opened to Ephesians. Daily and devout reading of the Bible was the habit of a lifetime of this good Protestant woman, who was loved and respected by all in Kincally parish. There wasn't a sectarian, anti-Catholic bone in her body.

When they sat down, Mrs. Johnson, wearing the compulsory apron of countrywomen, cautioned, "You took a fierce risk coming here. You could be shot on sight. What brings you?"

"The killing of Fr. Maguire."

"Ah, yes, I guessed it had to be that," lamented Mrs. Johnson. "He was a fine man and I am aware he and you were close friends."

Mac Ireland nodded.

"Mrs. Johnson, do you realize because you saw the killer, you now could be in danger. And them boys won't hesitate to kill you whether you are Protestant or not."

Alarm suddenly appeared on her face.

"Didn't the RUC warn you?" he asked.

He already knew the answer.

"No, not a word from them. They never came near me."

"You realize what that tells you, Mrs. Johnson?"

She nodded, "Yes, it must have been a government killing."

Then she began to sob gently. "Patrick, I haven't forgotten that in the last Troubles – during the 1956 IRA campaign – one of your brothers could have shot my husband, Willie, yet he let him go. Even though Willie had fired on him. But Willie was a B Special [the Protestant militia], and he was only doing his duty because your brother was in the IRA."

Patrick nodded. She had told him that story many times.

"And because of that," she continued, "I've always had a great respect for your family – even though you are Republicans, and we are Unionists: you're Green and we are Orange," she gently sighed.

"Mrs. Johnson, can you tell me if the man who ran from the Church had any distinguishing features?"

"Now that you've mentioned it, there was something wrong with his left ear."

"What do you mean, Mrs. Johnson?"

"It was as if someone shot part of his ear off."

"Why do you say that, Mrs. Johnson?"

"Willie's uncles were in the auxiliaries and one of them was shot up badly by Michael Collin's men in Cork in 1920. His ear was disfigured just like that man's. It is now only coming back to me because you are the only one who asked me about it."

"Anything else you can tell me before I head back

over the Border, Mrs. Johnson?"

"He was a couple of inches taller than yourself and a fine figure of a man. Patrick, if you intend to tangle with him, you better be careful. He's a man to be reckoned with, I fear."

Mac Ireland shook the nice Protestant woman's hand, and disappeared into the night, only pausing to pick up his handgun.

As he sped across the fields toward the Border, he kept thinking of the guy with the disfigured ear. "If I get a hold of the hoor, he will have greater problems than a bad ear," he promised himself.

Within an hour, he was back in his favorite dugout. He put his handgun down beside the Armalites and the AK-47s.

He then picked up his own personal AK-47, double-checking to make sure he had cleaned it properly. And, of course, he had – as always. Cleaning it was easy, and that was one of the reasons he liked it.

The Armalite was popular among many in the IRA. Mac Ireland, however, still preferred the AK-47. He had assiduously practiced and trained with it; read almost everything ever written about it; and knew it inside out.

AK stands for "Avtomat Kalashnikova," – Automatic Kalashnikov – after Mikhail Kalashnikov, the Russian who invented it. It was first produced in 1947, and, therefore, given the model number 47. It is one of the world's first true assault rifles, that is, a rapid-fire, magazine-fed automatic rifle for infantry use.

It is gas operated: it uses the high-pressure gas from the fired cartridge to push a piston attached to the bolt carrier, thus driving the action. The gas tube, visible above the barrel, has vents to allow the excess gas to escape.

The resulting energy provides the motion for unlocking the action, extraction of the spent case, ejection, cocking of the hammer, chambering of a fresh cartridge, and locking of the action.

It fires the 7.62x39mm cartridge at 600 rounds per minute.

The AK-47 had been manufactured by many countries and used by regular armies and revolutionaries.

Its half wood – half steel design and its curved (30-round) magazine made it readily recognizable.

It had inspired endless replication. Indeed, worldwide, more AK-type rifles have been manufactured than all other assault rifles combined.

Mac Ireland liked the safety switch and the selectors switch.

The safety switch serves two functions: it blocks dirt by covering the slot that the bolt-carrier-lever moves through when firing, and it prevents the weapon from being cocked. The selectors switch enabled one to choose semi-automatic (single-fire) or full automatic mode. In the semi-automatic mode, when the trigger is pulled, only one bullet is fired, and to fire another one, the trigger must be pulled again. In the automatic mode (the middle position), when the trigger is held down, bullets will keep firing until the magazine is empty or the trigger is released.

Mac Ireland would tape two magazine clips together for convenience so that he could more quickly reload.

Across the world, the AK-47 was legendary for its ruggedness and ability to fire no matter how wet or dirty.

That was important to Mac Ireland who spent so much of his time up to his neck in rivers, bog holes, ditches and sheughs (Northern Ireland lingo for ditches or drains brimmed with soft muck and God knows what).

Because of its large gas piston – and because its moving parts have lots of clearance – the weapon could tolerate the muck, mud and gravel of the Fermanagh-Cavan countryside without ever getting jammed or stuck.

However, those very same features reduced its accuracy, but that did not deter Mac Ireland. The AK-47 only weighed 9. 5 pounds (4.3 kg) when empty; 10.7 pounds (4. 9 kg) loaded. Its overall length is 34.21 inches (870 mm). The average service life of an AK-47 is 20 to 40 years.

Kevin O'Neill preferred the Armalite (AR-15, designated the M16 by the US military), and they had many spirited discussions about the pros and cons. O'Neill would emphasize that the Armalite was about a pound lighter and had a range of 670 yards (610 m) whereas that of the AK-47 was 440 yards (400 m).

However, they agreed to differ and each man held on to his preferred gun.

As Mac Ireland put his AK down again, he sat on the side of his bunk, and reflected on how critics of the Irish freedom-struggle liked to stereotype the IRA as being obsessed with guns. How come it was okay for the British and American soldier to be seen as reliant on his gun but not for the Irish soldier?

That led Mac Ireland to think of his other pet peeve: book covers about the IRA showing a gun and Rosary Beads. It was a double put down: scoffing at both the

Irish struggle and Catholicism.

When a picture appeared of a British or American soldier praying in a foxhole, it was somehow noble, indeed, touching – certainly not to be scoffed at. After all, everyone respected (if not accepted) the maxim, "There are no atheists in a foxhole." Yet, when the IRA man prayed in his foxhole or dugout, it was somehow presented as fanatical. Especially so, when the Rosary Beads were thrown into the mix. Now, this scoffing was not done by Jews or Muslims but by British Christians. Which raises the question: how could meditating on the Incarnation, Life, Death and Resurrection of Jesus Christ – which is what The Rosary is all about – be considered fanatical by alleged Christians? Why was that double standard never challenged?

Ironically, all that rumination reminded Mac Ireland to say his prayers before he climbed into bed. So down on his knees he went – whether British Christians liked it or not.

CHAPTER 5

When he woke in the morning, the man "with the bad ear" was still front and center of Mac Ireland's mind. Not only had he to track him down, he also had to figure out the connection between the killing of Fr. Maguire and the message the priest had sent him – "It's the 'Middle Name.'"

Already Mac Ireland knew what the "Middle Name" referred to. He and Fr. Maguire discussed three names they had written down on a piece of paper – the first name, the middle name and the last name. That was the sequence they had arranged to be used in messages between them. They would only refer to the order of the names and not to the names of the three individuals. Fr. Maguire would never have sent the message unless he had absolute certainty that the "Middle Name" was in fact, the informer, the British agent in the IRA, who had been responsible for many murders and so much treachery.

And to make the problem far worse, there was nobody Mac Ireland could turn to. The IRA had been seriously penetrated at the very top. There was nobody he could trust. There were many men and women who were totally trustworthy, but he didn't want to tell them in case the whole movement would implode resulting in deadly feuds. He knew he could no more bring the informer/agent before an IRA court than he could bring the Brit who killed Fr. Maguire before a British or Irish court. What does the just man do when he knows justice will not be done because of unjust political structures? It is not a question of taking the law into one's own hands because there is no law in this part of the world. And let no one trivialize the issue by dismissing it as vigilantism. It was on a different plane all together. These were the serious questions that Mac Ireland was pondering. However, he already knew what the proper course of action was.

Mac Ireland knew the IRA man who was "Middle Name." He had met him a number of times, yet never cared too much for him. He always felt there was something strange about him – something not quite right about him, yet he couldn't put his finger on it. What made the whole business really awful was that "Middle Name" was the man in charge of interrogating and executing suspected police informers and British agents within the IRA. This gave him unequaled power and access to the most closely guarded secrets of the IRA. It was the worst-case scenario for the IRA. Mac Ireland knew it was a deadly serious situation. If "Middle Name" was able to get into such a key position, it might mean that there were other British agents at the top of the IRA. Mac Ireland knew what he had to do. He got a secret and coded message delivered to "Middle Name" who alternated between Belfast and South Armagh: "Come to County Cavan to interrogate a suspected British agent."

"Middle Name" was Vini Fratelli (pronounced Fratell-i), a look-alike for a much smaller version of the old Italian-American movie star, Victor Mature. Fratelli was only 5' 9."

Fratelli's grandfather Louie was from the little town of Poggibonsi in Tuscany, Central Italy – 25.5 miles from Florence. He was a skilled stone and marble craftsman, who had emigrated to Belfast to work on the building of Clonard Church in West Belfast in 1908, and other notable structures in that city.

Vini's father, Dino, settled in West Belfast and Vini was born in 1938. He grew up – apart from his name and looks – a typical Belfast Catholic. In 1970 he joined the IRA. He was never much of a soldier, but he did have an aptitude for ferreting out information and for being able to quickly get the measure of a man. He was soon assigned to "internal security" – the section of the IRA that sought out and executed British agents and police informers in the ranks. He promptly made his mark, establishing himself as a feared and ruthless interrogator. ... But now exposed by Fr. Maguire as a paid agent of Her Majesty's Government.

Mac Ireland arranged to meet Fratelli in a safe house deep in the County Cavan countryside. He had two of his men pick him up in Cavan town. These two men were not in the IRA and the local IRA was not even aware of them. One of Mac Ireland's strengths was that the local people had total trust in him – even those who were not sympathetic to the IRA.

For special projects, Mac Ireland liked to use non-IRA members. It spread the responsibility and it freed up IRA men for strictly military operations.

Mac Ireland had cautioned the two men that what he

was asking of them was deadly dangerous – it could get them killed by the Brits, the Free State and even by the IRA. "Don't worry, Patrick. We answer neither to the Brits nor to the IRA – only to you."

Mac Ireland had already decided that he would not stand on ceremony; that he wouldn't beat around the bush. He knew Fratelli would not reveal anything, and he himself did not believe in torture. Therefore, he would have to keep it short and simple.

Fratelli arrived at the safe house just as darkness fell.

"How's the famous Fermanagh leader?" he asked.

"Not too bad," replied Mac Ireland, as he put his Smith and Wesson to the forehead of his startled visitor.

"What the fuck, Patrick. What the hell are you doing? I could have you shot for this."

"Like you've had so many good men shot before," replied Mac Ireland, " now your shooting days are over, you murderous traitor."

Then he added, "Fr. Maguire found you out and you had him killed."

With that, the studied calmness disappeared and there was a flicker of alarm in Fratelli's eyes.

Mac Ireland continued: "Because you cannot be brought to justice before a British or Irish court – even before an IRA court – you are going to be executed for crimes against the Irish people."

Then Mac Ireland opened the door and shouted, "Come on in men."

The two men came in, wearing gloves.

They quickly placed specially protected handcuffs on the prisoner that would not leave marks. They bundled him into the backseat of the car with one of them on either side, hand guns stuck in his ribs. Mac Ireland drove the car a couple of miles to one of the many lakes that dotted the Cavan countryside.

At the lake's edge, the two men lifted the handcuffed executioner to his feet and turned him virtually upside down. With strong farmer's hands, they held the quivering, squirming traitor face down in about six inches of water.

It was surprisingly simple.

Laryngospasm set in quickly – as the water entered his lungs, a spasm in the larynx sealed his airway resulting in asphyxiation.

Fratelli died without even mounting a struggle, his lungs filling with Cavan lake water within five minutes.

Mac Ireland couldn't help but be struck by the fierce irony of it all: The most feared man in the IRA dispatched by two simple farmers whose only other remotely similar experience would have been "dipping sheep" – putting the body of a sheep under a liquid solution to kill parasites.

Silently, the two men continued about their business. They removed the handcuffs, tossed the dead body in one of the little row boats by the lake shore, shoved off, and rowed the boat into the middle of the lake. Mac Ireland followed them in another little row boat. The men unceremoniously dumped the body of the British agent into the dark, deep waters and climbed into Mac Ireland's boat – shoving off the abandoned boat into the pitch blackness.

A few days later, as Mac Ireland had anticipated, it was reported that an unidentified body was discovered drowned in a Cavan lake. Foul play was not expected as the man appeared to have fallen out of a little boat that was drifting on the lake. Neither the British nor the IRA would be in a hurry to identify the dead man, Mac Ireland had bet.

CHAPTER 6

Mac Ireland travelled back from the lake by himself.

While he had certain sympathy for the British soldiers he had recently dispatched into eternity, he had absolutely no empathy for the drowned man.

Not only was "Middle Name" responsible for Fr. Maguire's death, he had also systematically executed innocent men he falsely alleged to be informers – sometimes even killing British informers to protect his own cover. And worst of all, he had been doing it for money. Whatever view one took of political violence – or the armed struggle, as the IRA preferred to call it – one surely had to recognize the distinction between fighting for your country's freedom and killing your own people for money.

Though he was sensitive to the terrible issue of violence – and indeed, powerfully attracted to the philosophy of nonviolence – he felt completely justified in bringing "Middle Name" to justice. "Here I stand; I can do no other, God help me. Amen," he wryly recalled Martin Luther's famous declaration on breaking with Rome.

When he got back to yet another one of his safe houses, there was a message waiting for him: The

Protestant women wants to meet you again.

"My goodness, my wife will begin to be suspicious" he laughed to himself. "Just as well Mrs. Johnson is in her 70s."

And then he reflected on how terrible his being on the run was for Mary. We could have such a lovely life together if our country were free. We could raise a wonderful family – teach them all the important things in life. How to be kind and just, how to build up "The Beloved Community" as Martin Luther King, Jr. taught, setting all religious differences aside and treating every one as our brother and sister in Christ. Wouldn't that be grand? But in the meantime, he and Mary would have to live on dreams deferred.

At times like this – and with thoughts like these – Mac Ireland could get sentimental and always the haunting lyrics of the old Irish ballad, "The Valley near Slievenaman" would flood his head and heart. Its author was that splendid old warrior-poet, Charles Kickham – a key leader of the IRB (Irish Republican Brotherhood) who died in 1882 at the early age of 54.

> *Alone, all alone by the wave-washed strand*
> *And alone in a crowded hall,*
> *The hall it is gay and the waves they are grand*
> *But my heart is not here at all,*
> *It lies far away by night and by day*
> *To the times and the joys that are gone*
> *But I never will forget the sweet maiden I met*
> *In the valley of Slievenamon*

Mac Ireland knew some "progressives" would regard that ballad as sentimental mush. But to hell with them boys; to him it was beautiful and charming. It annoyed him that in the 26-Counties, the "Dublin 4" mentality wanted to denigrate the fine old Irish ballads. (This area was seen by some as the snobbish, unpatriotic part of the city which had been designated as postal district number 4.).

Mac Ireland had to shake himself out of his reverie. Back to the Protestant woman, he told himself.

What is it about, he wondered. One thing is sure, I cannot risk going back to her farmhouse. I will have to get her to come over the Border into the Free State (that was also risky for him).

He arranged for her to check into a hotel in Cavan town. He slipped up the back stairs, tapped on her door and walked in.

"Mrs. Johnson, the Protestant Minister will be reprimanding you if we continue to meet like this," he joked.

She chuckled at that, and told him to sit down at a little round table in the corner of the room. She sat on the other straight-backed chair.

Mrs. Johnson pulled her glasses half way down her nose and, in her direct Protestant way, began.

"Patrick, do you remember my husband Willie's brother Sammy? He lived near your own townland of Derraliff before he moved to Belfast with his young family. You would have been a wee lad at the time."

"I do, indeed. Sure, his father used to cut my father's hair when my father was a young man. Whatever became of Sammy? Is he still alive?"

"Ah no, he's long dead. But here's why I've come to meet you. Sammy was successful in business and one of his sons became a very important man."

"What does he do?" asked Mac Ireland.

"He's a big shot in the police."

Mac Ireland immediately stiffened.

"Mrs. Johnson, where's this heading, please?"

"Wait now, Patrick, don't get excited. You realize, I would never play you false, despite our political differences."

"Ah, alright, Mrs. Johnson, I'm sorry. Please go ahead?"

"Sammy's son – his name is also Sammy – is about 40. I'm not sure what he does, except that it has to do with that top secret stuff one reads about."

Again Mac Ireland could feel his back stiffen, and all his well-tuned survival instincts go into top gear.

Then Mrs. Johnson really dropped the bombshell: "Sammy wants to meet you."

What the hell is going on here, he wondered as he moved quickly to the window to glimpse out.

"Mrs. Johnson, what are you trying to do to me?

"Sammy is prepared to meet you anywhere as long as you give your word to me that you will not have him harmed."

"Ha, but what about the harm he could do to me?"

"Patrick, look at me. You have my word he won't do you harm." She looked him straight in the eyes, in her direct Protestant way.

Instinctively, and with certainty, Mac Ireland knew she spoke with complete honesty. He knew he could trust this decent Protestant woman.

"But why does he want to meet me?"

"I'm not sure, except it has to do with the killing of Fr. Maguire."

That settled that. Any misgiving he might have had went out the window.

He stood up, grasped her hand. "Mrs. Johnson, I'll meet with Sammy. Set it up. However, tell him this – and you please also understand it clearly – if he dishonors his word, and yours, I will have him shot."

And then he was gone.

CHAPTER 7

A meeting with the Protestant detective was clearly a huge risk for Mac Ireland. It was the most unusual development ever in his life. He was certain it wasn't a set-up, yet, for the life of him, he couldn't figure it out. With all the recent stuff, he knew he couldn't go to the IRA high command; therefore, he was putting himself in immediate and deadly danger. The fact that he was the most trusted IRA leader in the whole of Ireland would not save him. If he were killed, nobody would ever know whether the bullet was from the Brits or the IRA. It's disheartening one has to fight on so many fronts. It wasn't supposed to be like this. Yet wasn't that the story of poor Ireland – oppression, manipulation, agents and informers? Well, nobody promised it was going to be easy. And he smiled warmly when he recalled his own father's philosophy of life: "When you enlist, you have to soldier!"

Mac Ireland reasoned that it would be out of the question to meet Sammy Johnson anywhere near the North. It was just too dangerous for both of them. He, therefore, decided it was best to meet in a big hotel in Dublin. He put on his most effective disguise: a smart business suit, an amazingly convincing wig, brown, and curly that completely changed his appearance. He was always amazed when he looked at himself in the mirror – his own mother wouldn't recognize him.

At the appointed time, 4 PM, Mac Ireland boldly walked into the lobby of the Gresham Hotel, took the elevator to the third floor, and knocked firmly on the door of Johnson's room. He could sense the detective looking at him through the peephole.

The door opened slowly and the well-modulated voice directed, "Come in, Patrick."

Mac Ireland immediately recognized the man in front of him as a Johnson – just like all the other men in the family. "This is a hardy boy," Mac Ireland noted to himself.

Johnson was 5'10", a bit swarthy-looking, with receding brown hair, large brown eyes, slight moustache, narrow sloping shoulders, thin but thick frame, no fat, all muscle.

Whereas Mac Ireland looked very Irish, Johnson could have passed for Russian or Eastern European.

Mac Ireland jokingly wondered to himself if Johnson had a "long heel," and nearly cracked up at the thought of it. (The longer he was away from home the more the old anecdotes and stories – "the bits" – appeared hilarious).

The "long-heel bit" was priceless. A Catholic neighbor of his in Kincally – whose Johnson's parents would have certainly known well – believed that Protestants had longer heels than Catholics: "If you don't believe me," she would insist, "the next time you see a Protestant take a close look at his heel. It juts back much further than the Catholic heel." And that from a woman who was really friendly with all her Protestant neighbors! Mac Ireland hoped he might one day be able to tell Johnson this old "pishogue" (a silly old wives' tale).

Johnson with great show and a knowing smile, opened his nicely tailored blue jacket – demonstrating that he was unarmed.

Mac Ireland did the same as he, too, smiled.

"Nice to meet a Kincally man," grinned Mac Ireland as he held out his hand.

"Indeed," replied Johnson as he firmly shook hands.

Mac Ireland took note of Johnson's large hand and its powerful grip.

"You look like all the Johnson men."

"So I'm told.

"Isn't this a strange turn of affairs?"

"Indeed," agreed Johnson. "Have a seat Patrick and I'll get right to the point."

"In your direct Protestant way," interjected Mac Ireland, with a laugh.

"Indeed … . Now, Patrick, in different circumstances and maybe not too far down the road, we may end up shooting each other. I'm sure we both understand that. I am sworn to uphold the State of Northern Ireland, you are sworn uphold a United Ireland."

Mac Ireland nodded assent at that basic statement of fact.

"However," continued the well-spoken and well-dressed detective, "I believe we can, with honor and fidelity, join forces on a particular case."

He paused and looked intently at Mac Ireland, weighing him up, as he carefully chose his words.

"Patrick, I have an 18-year-old son, Billy. Well, I had

... until he was murdered."

"I'm sorry to hear that. Was he in the police? Did we kill him?"

Johnson cleared his throat, took a sip of water from the small bottle on his table, and sighed deeply.

"No, the IRA did not kill him. Protestant paramilitaries did – the UPF (Ulster Protection Force). They killed him because he stood up to one of their leaders who tried to bully him. I told my son always to stand up to bullies – and I taught him how to fight. Maybe I taught him too well because in a minute he had flattened the bully – knocked him out with one punch. But then my son sealed his own fate by shouting for all to hear that the UPF leader was 'a scumbag drug dealer and a murderer. He killed the old Protestant woman down the road to cover up his drug dealing. And I have the evidence to prove it.' A short time later a UPF gang grabbed my son and beat him to death with iron bars.

At first I thought that was all there was to it: a revenge killing and the elimination of a possible witness.

Can you fathom my horror, as a loyal Ulsterman and a faithful servant of The Crown, when I discovered that the murder was ordered by a high ranking British counter–insurgency expert, and a key leader of the SAS in Northern Ireland?

He was able to order the slaughter of my son because the UPF leader, and his key associates are all British Agents and police informers, whom he has personally recruited. He is controlling them, paying them, and supplying them with weapons and information."

Johnson paused as if out of breath, the recounting of his son's slaying having taken its toll.

Then, he almost pleaded, "And, Patrick, despite the fact I'm supposed to be a hot shot detective – with all sorts of commendations – I cannot touch the killers. They are a protected species."

Mac Ireland, while sympathetic, nonetheless, started to interject to ask what it had to do with him, but Johnson silenced him with an outstretched hand.

"The SAS man is the same bastard who assassinated Fr. Maguire."

"Oh, Lord," gasped Mac Ireland as he got up to pace about the room, as was his habit when he was agitated.

"My God, Sammy, are you sure?"

"I am absolutely, one hundred per cent certain. It's my own son, after all, that we are talking about."

And then he almost broke, holding down his head as he whispered, "It's unbelievably painful. My heart is breaking every day. Loosing Billy would be like watching my father and mother being killed before my own eyes, over and over again. It's that bad. And there's nothing I can do. That English bastard has friends in high places. And you know what the last straw is? They are taking the bastard out of the North and have given him a nice, safe assignment at the British Embassy in Washington, D.C."

Ah, isn't that typical of British policy, Mac Ireland reflected. Historically, they have promoted British officials for crimes committed in Ireland. Except the crimes were always against Catholics. Now, however, a Brit is being promoted for covering up the killing of a young innocent Protestant lad (and, of course for killing a priest).

What's his name, Sammy?'

"His name is Charlie Shepherd," Johnson spat out.

Mac Ireland stopped pacing around the room. Put his hands on his hips and leaned back to stretch his back and release the tension in his neck. He looked at Johnson who seemed to have aged about 20 years in the past 15 minutes. He was slumped in his chair with his chin almost on his chest.

Mac Ireland went over to him, put his hand on his shoulder.

"Sammy, what is it you want from me?"

Johnson straightened his back, sat upright, the gloom somehow lifting off him.

"I knew if I didn't give you this information, there was no way you could find out the identity of Fr. Maguire killer – and there is absolutely no way you could discover that he had been assigned to the British Embassy in Washington."

Then it was his turn to stand up.

He faced Mac Ireland and with quiet intensity declared: "I am a loyal Ulsterman, a faithful servant of Her Majesty. I would defend British interests with my life. But I owe no allegiance to murderers and to bastards who cover up murders. That is not what I am loyal to. I want to bring that bastard to justice – the final court of justice – and I think it is in your interest to help me – without either of us betraying what we are sworn to uphold. It's bloody ironic, but it's damn true."

Mac Ireland was silent for a long time. He couldn't be sure how much Johnson knew about the English killer's other activities – about how he also handled "Middle Name." But Mac Ireland didn't want to open up that can of worms. It was not relevant to the issue at hand

and, furthermore, Johnson, even if he knew, would not reveal it. Johnson had spelled out his own honor code. He would only reveal that which was strictly relevant to his son's murder. That far, and no farther.

That was enough for Mac Ireland and enough for justice – at least for the search for justice to begin.

"Now, Patrick, I need to say this to you. You cannot take this bastard down by yourself."

Mac Ireland bristled a little bit as he was inclined to when challenged.

"Wait, now, Patrick, I am not challenging either your ability or determination. But remember, I'm a detective. I've read the massive file the Brits and the RUC have on you."

Mac Ireland winced a little bit. The irony of it all. Indeed, it is more surreal than ironic.

Johnson continued, "Patrick, don't get me wrong. I realize you are a hardy Kincally man, and a fierce guerilla fighter. However, the IRA was never much trained in hand to hand fighting. And I suspect that the only way to bring this guy down will be at close quarters and without guns."

"Don't worry, I'll fix the hoor if I get hold of him." (except Mac Ireland pronounced it as if the word "hold" was spelled "howlt," in the way of Kincally folk).

Johnson smiled at the expression. It brought back a lot of memories. It was just the way his father spoke.

Then, he put both hands on Mac Ireland's shoulders and with the quiet intensity, he almost whispered: "Patrick, look at me, and listen to me. You will not be able "to fix him." He is the toughest bastard in the entire British Special Forces. He can kill you with his bare hands. I have been a champion boxer in the British armed services for many years – and before I joined the service, I was the champion street fighter in Protestant Belfast – and in the past, I would not have felt I could get the better of him. Now, however, because he's covered up the murder of my son, I may have the edge and I think I can put him down with two or at least three punches. And, Patrick, you would have no chance at all in a hand to hand confrontation."

As the two men stood eyeball to eye ball, Mac Ireland recognized that Johnson was not just indulging in some Protestant bravado or machismo. He could tell he knew what he was talking about. Furthermore, he was aware that he himself was no Rocky Marciano in a fist fight. Indeed, IRA men were always under orders never to get into such fights. And because Catholics – at least in the country area – did not have gyms or boxing clubs, they were not schooled in the boxing ring, least of all in street fighting.

Mac Ireland moved back from Johnson and sat back down on the chair. Putting his legs straight out, he crossed his ankles, showing his dark socks.

"I see. So where does that leave us?"

"At the British Embassy in Washington."

"What do you mean?"

"You and I, Patrick, have to go to Washington and take the bastard down in the "land of the free, and the home of the brave.""

And then with a show of feigned slyness, he smiled, "Have you ever been to America, Patrick?" Johnson was fully aware from his intelligence briefings that Mac Ireland had slipped in and out of America many times over the years to rally Irish-Americans to The Cause.

Patrick let the little dig slide.

"Why do we have to go to Washington? Why don't we get him in The North?"

But Johnson was ahead of him,

"I have seen the paper work (don't ask how). He won't be back in Britain or Ireland for at least five years. They realize the only way to keep him safe is to give him diplomatic immunity and keep him in America ... just like you keep some of your lads safe," he added in another mischievous dig.

This time Mac Ireland acknowledged the dig and smiled broadly. "I thought Protestants were meant to be direct – and not sly hoors," he parried.

Johnson threw his head back laughed at the wonderful irony of it all.

But Mac Ireland quickly became serious again.

"Sammy, I will help on one condition. I have learned there is a British agent at the top of the IRA – in a political position. I am not sure who it is. If you will reveal him – and I believe with your connections, you can – I will help you to take down Shepherd."

Johnson mulled this over for a long time.

"Patrick, I don't think I can. I could lose my job."

"What do you think could happen by your killing Shepherd? You could certainly lose your job for that, and I could lose my life on the streets of Washington. Anyway, Sammy, that's the way it is. If you don't give up the agent in The Movement, I will not help you, and Shepherd will remain untouchable."

And with that, Mac Ireland headed for the door.

"Hold on now, Patrick, wait a second." Mac Ireland

paused, turned around, and faced Johnson.

"Okay, Patrick, I'll do it if I can get the information."

"And with your connections, I am certain that you can. You must get the information to me before we go to Washington. Furthermore, I will not be able to go to Washington for at least two weeks after you have given me the information."

"Fair enough, Patrick, I'll go to work on it right away."

Mac Ireland shook his hand and moved toward the door again. Just before he opened it, he turned: "Sammy, you do realize if you try to deceive me, and finger the wrong man, then the pledge I gave to your aunt, Mrs. Johnson, is voided. And I will have you killed, no matter how long it takes."

"Yes, Patrick, I realize that. You have my word. I will not play you false."

"Finally, before I go, let me mention this: your aunt saw Shepherd leave the church. You, more than most, must understand that that puts her in real danger".

"Oh, I am acutely aware of that, Patrick. She told me that you had advised her of the danger".

Mac Ireland gave him a quick salute with his right hand, and quickly left the room.

Ten days later, Mac Ireland got the information from Johnson. Had he been sitting down, he'd have fallen off his chair. It was absolutely stunning. Emmet Mulligan, one of the most respected leaders in The Movement – both militarily and politically – had been a long time British agent.

Mac Ireland was devastated. In his wildest dreams, he would never have believed it. He had known Mulligan for many years. They had built bombs together and had shot British soldiers together. This man had sent others out to kill and maim. He was one of the most popular men in the Irish Republican Movement. He was a Gaelic speaker, a competent historian, and a former famous footballer. How could this be possible?

Of course, Mac Ireland understood how it was possible, because the British had always succeeded in infiltrating Irish revolutionary organizations – the Fenians in America and their Irish counterpart, the Irish republican Brotherhood, in the 1860s, and the IRA in the 1920s, 40s, 50s, and right up to the present. Indeed, he knew for certain that a former Chief of Staff firmly believed that the 1956 IRA Campaign had been sabotaged from America – that the main gunrunner then, and for years later, had been working all the time for the FBI.

Mac Ireland also realized that this case was far more complicated than that of "Middle Name," who was strictly on the military side and unknown to the general public. This agent, however, was one of the best-known men in Ireland. He had impeccable credentials, and his entire extended family was involved in The Movement. Exposing him as a British agent – even if it were possible – would cause enormous harm to The Movement. On the other hand, it would cause even more harm – indeed, the defeat of The Movement – if the agent were left in place.

"God, I didn't sign up for this. I never dreamt I'd be killing IRA men, but that's the point: they are not IRA men – they're British agents."

Mac Ireland's head was spinning with all this stuff.

He had to get off by himself.

He had picked up the coded message sent by Johnson in a hotel near Ballinamore. He now headed for another dugout that nobody knew about. It was where he went to do his most serious thinking

And yet, as always, Mac Ireland knew it was a foregone conclusion. He knew what he would have to do. Only he had the vital intelligence. It was his duty to right the situation. And this time, he knew he could not involve anyone else. It was too dangerous and too risky. This time, the only person he could trust was himself.

"I cannot tell a single soul. I'm utterly on my own. If I mess it up, I will be branded a terrible traitor to The Cause to which I have dedicated my life."

Mac Ireland knelt by his bunk, prayed his Rosary, and slipped into his bed. Despite the turmoil in his head, he was soon fast asleep. Prayer always calmed him down.

CHAPTER 8

Mac Ireland got a secret message back to Johnson that he would need further intelligence to be able to bring Mulligan to justice.

He needed to find out the next time Mulligan was meeting with his Brit-handler. Mac Ireland reminded Johnson that if he wanted Mac Ireland's help in Washington, he had to deliver this intelligence.

Johnson called him on a safe line and told him that Mulligan would be next meeting his handler in a small hotel at Carrybridge – the bridge to the east of the island of Inishmore that links the island to the Enniskillen road. It is midway on the Erne water system, near the small village of Lisbellaw.

Mulligan's handler was based in the Enniskillen RUC barracks. Mulligan himself was from County Down. Mac Ireland knew the Carrybridge area well, having been born on the banks of Lough Erne.

Johnson explained the agent and his handler would be meeting without any back–up from the Brits or the RUC. He assured Mac Ireland that he would get back to him with more details; nevertheless, he knew for certain the meeting would be in two weeks' time.

Mac Ireland figured that would give him enough

time. Already a plan was forming in his mind.

As a young man, Mac Ireland had plied the waters of Upper Lough Erne in a rowboat – visiting relatives, shooting and fishing. He felt totally at home on the water – it was, he claimed, where God spent most of His time.

He was fully aware of the danger that once he killed the agent and his handler, all the roads might be blocked within minutes – especially the roads leading to the Cavan border and the Free State. Still, his old friend – the waters of his home Lough – would provide safe passage. And it would be nice – apart from the danger and seriousness of the mission – to be back on the waters of his beloved Lough Erne. (He would have been the first to admit that that was an ironic thing for him to be thinking. However, he had long since learned to deal with danger and stress by reflecting on the ironic.).

Lough Erne – consisting of Upper and Lower – is really a widened section of the River Erne, which rises in County Cavan, flows north, then bends west, and empties into the Atlantic at Ballyshannon, County Donegal.

Upper Lough Erne, the southern-most Lough, is further up the river. Lower Lough Erne is further down the river (nearer the ocean) and more northern.

The Lough is 40 miles (64 km) long, has an average width of 5 miles (8 km), and a maximum depth of 200 feet (60 m).

Upper Lough Erne is shallow and 12 miles (19 km) long, and Lower Lough Erne, is deeper and 18 miles (29 km) long. They are connected by the 10-mile (16-kilometre) River Erne-strait.

Sitting astride the Upper and Lower Lough is the

island town of Enniskillen (Inis Ceithleann – Kathleen's Island), named after the ancient warrior Kathleen.

The island was captured by the English in 1607. The Plantation of Ulster followed during which the lands of the native Irish were confiscated and handed over to planters loyal to the English Crown. The Maguires were supplanted by William Cole, originally from Devon, who was appointed by James I to build an English settlement there.

Mac Ireland knew he would need the help of Seamus Reilly, who had brought him the fateful message from Fr. Maguire. Seamus was not actually in the IRA, but was someone Mac Ireland trusted implicitly. He was certain Reilly would never betray him. He would get Reilly to drive him part of the way to the shore of Lough Erne, and he would travel back on his own.

When Johnson confirmed the date, time and the room number of the meeting, Mac Ireland went into full operational mode. He packed his backpack, a small bottle of water, a pair of gloves, his night vision binocular goggles, courtesy of a contact in the U.S. military. He wasn't aware of any other IRA man who had those binoculars. Then he added a brown wig, a baseball cap and a light rain jacket. Last of all, he put in his Browning HP, single action, 9 mm semi-automatic pistol, with its 13-round magazine capacity. In Ireland, some referred to this handgun as a BAP (Browning Automatic Pistol). It was his French-speaking wife, Mary, who first explained to him that when the pistol was referred to as a GP, it was because of the French term, "Grande Puissance"(major power). He finally added the silencer for his "major power" – and the backpack was complete for his mission.

On the appointed evening, Mac Ireland crossed the side of the mountain and followed the river down to the back of Reilly's farm. Seamus was already waiting for him in the car. They drove for two miles to a junction on the main road to Enniskillen. Mac Ireland, who had made sure to put on his gloves before he got into the car, thanked Seamus, slipped out of the car. When the car had disappeared, Mac Ireland cut across a few fields, slid down the right bank of the river, and waded over to the left side of the river, climbing up on its bank. He followed the river to the mouth of Lough Erne where a small but efficient 16-foot motorboat was waiting, hardly visible among the bulrushes.

Mac Ireland made a quick check. The keys were in the ignition. The petrol tanks were full and, importantly, a pair of sturdy oars. By now it was around 9 P.M., and beginning to get dark. He knew he could easily make it to Carrybridge in thirty minutes.

The motor purred beautifully and sprang into life. Mac Ireland took off slowly until he was in deeper water, and then he increased the speed to about ten knots. It was a beautiful evening, and Mac Ireland recalled how his father – God rest him – loved these waters. And how they had often fished and duck-hunted in some of the very spots he was now motoring past. Of course, in those days they were not using a motor boat, just a row boat. His father was a skilled oars-man and could glide along the water almost as fast as a small motor boat. He would tell folk that he was never worried about being on the Lough in the pitch darkness because all he had to do was put his finger in the water and he could tell his location exactly – even though the Upper Lough is a maze of little islands. Apparently folk believed him, too!

But then boys from the Erne could always sling a good line of BS. ... as displayed by the beloved traditional song, "Buchaill on Eirne" (Boy from the Erne).

"Buachaill ón Éirne mé's bhréagfainn féin cailín deas óg.

Ní iarrfainn bó spré léithe tá mé féin saibhir go leor.

'S liom Corcaigh 'a mhéid é, dhá thaobh a' ghleanna's Tír Eoghain.

'S mura n-athraí mé béasaí's mé n't-oidhr' ar Chontae Mhaigh Eo.

(I'm a boy from the Erne and I could charm a nice young girl.

I would not ask for her wealth, as I am rich enough myself.

I own a good part of Cork, two sides of the glen in Tyrone And not to repeat myself, I'm the heir of County Mayo)."

However, this is not the song of a braggart, but a tongue-in-cheek, flirtatious and teasing song sung to his loved one. Mary would melt his heart every time she would sing it for him, and to him. One day, please God, she would be able to sing it to him in the very place where he was now motoring along – but in happier times, peaceful ones: in an Ireland free from the center to the sea, from the sod to the sky.

"But back to the mission," Mac Ireland now reminded himself.

When he was about a mile away from Carrybridge, Mac Ireland shut off the engine, put the key in his pocket, slipped the oars into their spurs, and rowed gently to the left hand shore. He jumped out of the boat and pulled it onto land, leaving it hidden in the bulrushes.

The water was cold on his boots, but he had decided against wearing wellingtons because they would slow him down.

Once the boat was secure, Mac Ireland took out his night vision glasses and swept the area. Everything looked fine. He quickly and cautiously darted toward the hotel, and hid among the bushes. He still had some time because the two targets would not meet until 10 P.M. He put on his brown wig, baseball cap, and gloves. He scouted the area carefully. It hadn't changed all that much since he had gone on the run – except there were now ten small rooms added with the doors facing the lough. These rooms were favored by fishermen who were not interested in hotel amenities, but only with a bed for the night.

Johnson had told him that the meeting was being held in the end room as he came up from the lough. He had also told him that the door was flimsy with no real lock. Furthermore, he added, "Those boys have become so arrogant that they probably won't even bother locking the door. Besides, the hotel is only used by Protestant customers and English fishermen, so it is considered a safe haven for such a meeting."

Mac Ireland put the night vision binoculars in his backpack, hoisted it on his shoulders, and got ready.

At exactly 10 P.M., Mac Ireland saw a middle-aged man approach the end room and enter. About four minutes later, he saw a younger man approach. At first he didn't recognize him in his Irish cap and long hair. Then he quickly realized Mulligan was wearing a wig.

"How could he do this? How could the bastard betray his comrades and his country?"

With that, Mac Ireland realized he had to take deep breaths and calm down because he was feeling righteous anger boil up.

He waited for five more minutes. He was betting the handler would be the one who was armed. Mulligan would not be armed in case he were stopped on his way to the meeting. Because if he were stopped and searched, the regular RUC man or British soldier would have no idea he was a British agent. So Mac Ireland knew the moment he entered the room he would have to first shoot the Brit handler, and then execute Mulligan.

He also knew he couldn't indulge in the much loved movie devise – having dialogue with his two targets. There would be no beautifully sculpted words, no exchange, and no meaningful glances. He would go in there, shoot them both and immediately disappear into the Lough Erne night.

As Mac Ireland gently turned the door knob, he realized that Johnson was right – the arrogant bastards had not even bothered to push in the little lock button on the inside of the door knob. Realizing it was unlocked, he quickly stepped inside.

The two men were sitting at a small table along the side of the right-hand wall, sideways to the door. Mulligan yelled, "What the fuck – it's Mac Ireland." Mac Ireland ignored him, pointed his HP with silencer at the Brit-handler, and shot him twice in the heart and then in the head. He calmly turned his gun on Mulligan (who had spun around to face him, eyes glaring in fear) and shot him two times in heart and once in the head. It only took a few seconds, with little or no commotion.

Mac Ireland didn't even pause to check if they were dead. He knew they were.

He turned on his heel and walked out of the room, closing the flimsy door behind him. Nobody was walking about in the area. He strode at a sharp, unhurried pace, climbed down the side of the riverbank, and off to the boat.

He shoved the boat off the ground into the shallow water and rowed silently for about a half mile. Once out in the open water, safely away from the possibility of anyone hearing the motor, he turned on the engine and headed back the way he came.

It was now quite dark, though that didn't bother Mac Ireland who knew this part of Lough Erne like the back of his hand. When he was in the deepest water, he dropped his gun and silencer overboard.

Within a half hour Mac Ireland parked the boat. He took out the little cloth from his backpack and swabbed down the boat as best he could. "It's the law of the water – always clean down the boat after use, especially when it belongs to someone else."

Mac Ireland followed the river all the way across the border. When he was a boy, he could do that so easily because there were no barbed wire fences in those days – just hedges. Now, however, he had to slip into the river and wade or swim to get past some difficult fences. This time, he didn't take his boots because had about eight miles of hard walking to do – and in the dark. In about two hours, Mac Ireland was safely back in one of his dugouts. He sat on his bunk and removed his soaked boots. "I've just executed one of the best known

IRA men in the country. Or at least someone who was perceived as an IRA patriot. What will happen now? He wondered if the Brits would admit the dead handler was one of theirs. And he just couldn't figure out how the Republican Movement would handle it. Surely they would have to wonder what a man from County Down was doing in a "Protestant hotel" at that time of night. One thing he was certain of, however, was that he could never talk to anyone about it – until he was certain he was not talking to yet another British agent. He also knew if it ever got out, he was a dead man – killed by the Brits or even by well-meaning IRA men or women who simply would not believe that Emmet Mulligan could be a British agent and informer.

CHAPTER 9

When Mac Ireland woke up the following morning, he knew he would have to take some time off, and get away from the Border. Furthermore, he had promised his long-suffering wife, Mary, that he would take her to Dublin for a few days.

He made arrangements for Mary to get a "safe" car – one that would not be on the Guards or Special Branch watch list.

Mary picked up Mac Ireland in a safe house outside Ballyconnell. At first, she almost didn't recognize him – all dressed up in sports coat and pants, wearing his brown wig that almost came down to his shoulders. With black heavy framed glasses, he looked every inch of the modern professor.

Mary herself was no shrinking violet. She wore black pants, red top and dangerous looking high heels. "How are you going to drive in them heels?" he grinned, but quickly followed up with, "You look wonderful."

"Okay, you've redeemed yourself," she beamed. "Now, professor, in you get. Remember, you are not allowed to cast aspersions on my shoes."

"It would take me a whole year to do that, you have so many," he quipped back, smiling broadly. Mary laughed loudly, and proudly.

They motored at a safe speed so as not to attract police attention, driving through Belturbet and Cavan town. After an hour and a half, they arrived in the historic town of Kells, which Mac Ireland always liked. They stopped in Kells and had tea and biscuits in a hotel.

During the tea, they reminisced about their only other real break, away together: their five-day honeymoon in Salthill, Galway. They stayed in a Bed and Breakfast on Whitestrand Road, with a perfect view of Galway Bay. It gave them a new insight into the appeal of the old song, composed by Dr. Arthur Colahan in 1947, "Galway Bay."

> *"If you ever go across the sea to Ireland,*
> *Then maybe at the closing of your day,*
> *You will sit and watch the moon rise over Claddagh*
> *And see the sun go down on Galway Bay…"*

Mary sang it beautifully to Patrick each time they watched the moon rise, and saw the sun go down.

And this fierce guerilla fighter would melt, thinking his heart would burst with love for his Cavan bride.

However, he had always wondered about the fourth verse of the song:

> *"For the strangers tried to come and teach us their*
> *   way*
> *They scorned us just for being what we are;*
> *But they might as well go chasing after moonbeams*
> *Or light a penny candle from a star."*

Patrick knew that the author, Dr. Colahan, had been born in Enniskillen, and that made him proud. On the other hand, the good doctor had been an officer in the British Army. He didn't feel too proud of that. However, wasn't it interesting the Colahan could write about "the strangers tried to come and teach us their way" when, in fact, he had belonged to the very army that had attempted to do that "teaching" – at the point of a bayonet? Ah, the conflicted soul of some Irishmen!

Mary and Patrick had gone to Mass in St. Mary's of the Claddagh near Longwalk,

They visited St. Nicholas's Church to see the alleged imprint of Cromwell's horse's hoof print.

They snacked at Griffin's bakery.

Patrick bought Mary a modest piece of jewelry at Dillon's: a delicate yellow gold-link bracelet with stones of Connemara Marble.

They had a beautiful time.

"Mary, this is wonderful. I realize it is very simple. Rich folk would not consider it much, but to me it's glorious."

"I'm rich folk, Patrick, and that means you are, too!"

"Well, yes love, but you know what I mean."

She dissolved into peals of laughter. Patrick found it difficult to accept he "had married into money." She delighted in his cognitive dissonance, and teased him gleefully about it.

Still, she was careful not to overdo it. She was very aware that on a deeper level Patrick was grateful she was rich – it eased his guilt about not being able to provide any financial support. Mary, however, was very direct about this.

"Patrick, you win our freedom from England, and I will take care of the finances. We are blessed to be in this position. I will secure our family's future; you secure our country's freedom." (They had deliberately kept the honeymoon simple so as not to attract attention).

They would walk for miles along Galway Bay. Naturally, they had to make a pilgrimage to Teach a Phiarsaigh (Pearce's cottage) – the small thatched cottage that Patrick Pearse used as a summer residence and school.

With both of them loving the water, there was no way they were going to miss out on boat tour of Galway Bay and down to the Cliffs of Moher. Nor the thirty-mile boat trip to Aran Island, where Mary could show off her perfectly fluent Irish to all the native speakers.

Before they left the island, they had a cold seafood dish in a restaurant right by the water's edge. "This is the greatest seafood I've ever tasted in my life," gushed Mary to the waiter. "If it's not fresh here, then it's not fresh anywhere in the world," he responded with island pride.

And that's how their tea-time passed in Kells – reliving their honeymoon in Galway. But now it was time to continue to Dublin.

When they got back into the car, Mac Ireland suggested, "Mary, you've never been to Glasnevin Cemetery and you've always wanted to. Let's do it on the way up. It's only about two miles north of the city center".

"That sounds lovely, and what will we do in Dublin?

"I hope we will be able to get tickets for a play at the Abby Theatre and the Gate."

"Wonderful," exclaimed Mary – thoroughly enjoying their excellent adventure.

"Mary, you realize I feel really bad about what you have to put up with. You are terrific about it, but I know how tough it is for you."

"Patrick, we both knew the reality of the situation before we married. You are dedicated to Ireland's Cause. I am proud of you and I support you one hundred per cent. Don't worry about me. I'm a strong, independent Cavan woman. I can handle it."

Mac Ireland choked up. What a splendid wife he had. She was intelligent, beautiful and determined.

Mary reached out for his hand, "Now, professor, let's relax and enjoy ourselves. No more serious talk."

Mac Ireland smiled and leaned back in his seat. In about an hour and a half, they were parking outside Glasnevin Cemetery. It was one of Mac Ireland's favorite spots in the whole of Ireland. Although well over a million people were buried there, for him Glasnevin was not so much a cemetery as a national monument to Ireland's patriot dead. It's Ireland's Arlington Cemetery (where Jack and Bobby Kennedy are buried).

Mac Ireland was like a schoolboy with excitement at the prospects of giving his Mary a guided tour of this special spot. As they entered the cemetery, he immediately pointed to the massive 150-foot monument to Daniel O'Connell, the Liberator. Then he first brought her to the grave of one of his greatest heroes – John Devoy (1842-1928) whom Patrick Pearse rightly predicted would be remembered as the greatest of all the Fenians. Devoy would go on to become the powerful leader of Clan na Gael in America.

At Devoy's grave, both he and Mary automatically knelt and said a prayer.

"He was a hardy man, Mary. Indomitable, unbreakable and fiercely intelligent. Ireland never produced a finer patriot."

Mary nodded, deeply touched by the earnestness and devotion of her husband.

Then Mac Ireland excitedly enthused, "Come now, Mary, and I'll show you the monument to the other great Irish-American Fenians, including John O'Mahoney, the Fenians founder, and Terence Bellew Mc Manus, the Young Irelander, whom my father always claimed was a relative of ours, on his mother's side.

For hours and hours, they walked from one historic monument to another. Finally, Mac Ireland suggested it was time to leave.

"Patrick, Sweetheart, that was a marvelous experience. I can't believe I had never been here before".

In about an hour, they were checking into a modest, yet comfortable, little hotel just off O'Connell Street.

"In the morning, Mary, we will have to pay our respect to the GPO."

They had a light supper and retired for an early night. Over the next few days, they had an absolutely marvelous time seeing all the sights in Dublin. They took in Ibsen's play *A Doll's House* **at** The Abbey and O'Casey's play *The Shadow of a Gunman at The Gate*.

One day they drove across the Dublin Mountains into Glendalough ("Gleann Da Loch," Valley of Two Lakes) in County Wicklow.

Glendalough is the famous monastic settlement founded by St. Kevin who died in about 618. For about six hundred years it flourished as one of Ireland's most important monastic centers, until the English/Normans destroyed it in 1398.

It was one of Mac Ireland's favorite trips (as long

as there was no fog that often could make sightseeing impossible). The other thing he loved about the trip was that the return trip, on the same road, somehow looked entirely different. Mac Ireland and Mary were in their element driving through all the barrenness and heather.

"Patrick, Sweetheart, even though we don't get to spend much time together, no couple could have a better time than we have."

That delighted Mac Ireland's warrior heart. My God, he thought, I have a wonderful wife. When Ireland is free, I will make it up to her.

• • • • • •

Five days later, Mac Ireland was back in a safe house about three miles from The Border. He sent for Packie and told him to assemble the unit for a meeting the following evening at 9 P. M.

Kevin and the others showed up on time.

"Eamon," grinned Patrick, "you are not going to have time to discuss theology and religion this evening."

"Ah, that's alright, Patrick. I'll get you some other time," smiled Eammon as he shook Mac Ireland's hand.

Kevin, who had assumed command in Mac Ireland's absence, gave a summation of the Unit's activity "Our sniper killed one British soldier, and wounded two more. We got a RUC Special Branch man as he tried to cross The Border. And one of our men killed an RUC man as he drove his car from Kincally to the Enniskillen road."

Then he stopped and looked around at the others: "However, the real issue that everybody is talking about is the killing of Emmet Mulligan and that Brit at Carrybridge. Nobody's sure what to make of it."

He then added, "Patrick, do you have anything to

say about this?"

"No, Kevin. I'm as much at a loss as everyone else. I'm just not sure what to make of it. I just think we will have to wait and see what the statement of the Leadership says. Though one thing is perfectly clear, things are ratcheting up. All of you now are in clear and present danger. Kevin, I am not going to be around for a while. You men have done great in my absence, but because of the ways things are escalating, I think our Flying Column should play it cool for a while. Take some time off. Rest up and come back ready for action when things have cooled off. This is going to be a long war. And we have to take a long-headed view of it, so to speak."

They all got to their feet, shook Mac Ireland's hand and separately disappeared into the Cavan night.

Mac Ireland realized he also had to keep a low profile – and he had to make preparations for his Washington Mission.

He telephoned Johnson from a safe line and they discussed arrangements.

CHAPTER 10

A few days later, Mac Ireland was in a safe house in the center of Dublin making arrangements for his visit to Washington.

He had decided he would not go through any of the usual contacts in Irish America. They were fine people – the salt of the earth, in the Fenian tradition – but a priest friend in Washington had warned him that the Irish-American groups were heavily penetrated. "And not just by the Brits or the FBI, but by the Free State as well," the priest had told him. "In fact, the Free State has their spies in every Irish nationalist group in America. Even more so than the Brits."

The priest had also offered to put up both he and Johnson in the monastery when they come to Washington. The priest had no idea why this "odd couple" was coming to Washington, nor did he wish to find out. He told Mac Ireland on the phone, "It will be nice having an Ulster Protestant in the house. Remember Patrick, I've always told you every good Catholic needs a good dose of Protestantism."

Mac Ireland had passed on the priest's invitation to Johnson. "It's a good place for us to camp out. Nobody will notice us there. It's a large monastery-church near the National Mall at the bottom of Capitol Hill."

Mac Ireland knew The Capitol Hill location would attract Johnson's attention. Johnson had previously told him that although the Englishman worked at the British Embassy, he lived on Capitol Hill and ran each morning on The National Mall.

"I'll see you in Washington, Sammy," Mac Ireland replied as he hung up the phone.

Mac Ireland flew into Toronto and was taken over the Canadian-U.S. border by friends. He stayed the night in Niagara Falls. In the morning, he was picked up by the other friends and brought to a small airport and flown on a small private plane to Washington, D.C.

Mac Ireland was fascinated each time he saw an aerial view of the Nation's Capital. The magnificent Potomac river, the Kennedy Center, the majestic Lincoln Memorial, the splendid National Mall, all the way up to the unparalleled beauty of the U.S. Capitol, not to mention the White House. He would have loved to have been able to live in Washington. How different his life would have been. The National Mall was a far cry from the Fermanagh-Cavan Mountains where he had spent most of the past seven years on the run. Man, he thought, Mary would love it here. Maybe one day we will be able to visit. Then he snapped out of his day dreaming, conscious again of the gravity of the situation. He was coming into Washington to bring to justice a killer who was protected by the British Government, and now enjoyed the full protection that the United States provided when it granted diplomatic immunity.

Taking action against a British diplomat in America was a deadly serious business. Not only would it meet with universal condemnation, it could alienate even the most ardent IRA supporters in Irish America. Of course, it would not be the IRA taking action. The IRA weren't even aware of it so they could honestly deny they were involved. This is definitely my most dangerous mission, Mac Ireland told himself. Yet, he didn't have the slightest doubt about its rightness. It violates all sorts of laws, but it is right, he assured himself. Anyway, there was no going back now. Yet he hated the idea of being shot down on the streets of Washington by American law officials who would be only doing their duty. Being shot by the Brits in Fermanagh is something I can accept, even expect, but being killed by Americans ... that would kill me altogether!

Before long, the small plane was on the ground and he was soon out of the Washington airport. Fr. Terence Murphy picked him up and drove him to the monastery. Fr. Murphy was in his seventies, and had known Mac Ireland's father well.

"You look like your father, Patrick." "When can we expect your Protestant friend?"

"Probably in a couple of days."

"The monastery's rooms are simple, a bed, a chair and a table."

"Don't worry, Father, that will do me fine. As you can imagine, I am not used to luxury."

Mac Ireland then explained to the priest that while he was staying at the monastery, he would be wearing a disguise.

"Whatever you need to do."

Fr. Terence was unusually tall for men of that generation – 6′3″.

In the 1940s and 50s in Kincally the old folk would still talk in amazement about, "a big six-footer."

In the 50s when Fr. Terence would come home on vacation to Derraliff, he would delight the younger Mac Ireland children by giving them half-crowns – a mighty sum of money to an Irish child in those days. The children would count the days until they came back the following summer.

Fr. Murphy was born across the field from the home of Mac Ireland's parents in the town land of Derraliff. He had immigrated to America as a young man, became a cop and then finally entered the priesthood. He had over the years become, in effect, the Chaplain in Chief, so to speak, to practically every Irish cop up the entire East Coast of the U.S. Those cops had kept telling him if he ever needed any help, especially if it had to do with Ireland, all he had to do was to call.

Fr. Murphy began to feel that somehow he might need to make that call because he could sense that Mac Ireland was on some dangerous mission, but why would a Protestant from Belfast be coming with him? He didn't want to know. But one thing was sure, he would help the son of his closest neighbor across the field in Derraliff, especially since that son had dedicated his life to Irish freedom. He would do it willingly, with a clean conscience and no questions asked.

After all, hadn't the Redemptorist Order in Boston put up Dev when he was on the run in 1919-1920?

Before they got out of the car at the monastery, Patrick slipped on his wig, and put on a pair of glasses giving him an academic, professorial appearance.

Fr. Murphy looked at him and smiled.

"I'm thinking, Patrick, it might be best if I tell the other priests and brothers in the monastery that you are a Christian Brother from Ireland. In that way, there won't be too much notice taken of you. Religious folk pass through here all the time."

Mac Ireland laughed. "What do I tell them I teach?"

"Can you bluff your way on religion and Irish history?"

Mac Ireland chuckled, "In my sleep; I can do it in my sleep. What can we invent for the Protestant heretic, Sammy Johnson, to teach?" he chuckled.

"You told me he's a fit boy who boxes and that sort of thing. So let's say he is a teacher of physical education."

"That's grand. We are now so deep under cover The Vatican could not even uncover us."

Fr. Murphy laughed though he knew The Vatican probably wouldn't find it at all funny.

In the morning, Mac Ireland was up early and attended Mass in the monastery oratory. He felt wonderful to be able to celebrate the Eucharist without fear of arrest. After a light breakfast, he went for a two-hour walk on The National Mall.

The National Mall is absolutely not a shopping mall. Rather, it is a huge, open green space, an urban park (indeed, a national park). It comprises 684 acres and is lined by 2,000 American elm trees. It is sometimes called," The Nation's front yard."

Officially, The National Mall stretches from the U.S. Capitol to 14th St. N.W. Most commonly, however, it is regarded as stretching all the way to the Lincoln Memorial – a distance of 1.9 miles (3.0 km). It is bordered by Constitution and Pennsylvania Avenues on the north, and by Independence and Maryland on the south. It has a standard width of 1500 feet (457.2 m) but narrows to about 500 feet (152.4 m) near The Capitol.

The Mall forms the political and cultural heart of the Nation's Capital. It contains some of the nation's most cherished and treasured memorials and landmarks: the Lincoln Memorial, the Jefferson Memorial, the Washington Monument, etc. etc. It is lined by world famous museums of the Smithsonian Institution. And it forms the perfect stage for national expressions of remembrance, celebrations and – very importantly – protests and the exercise of First Amendment Rights. The most notable example of the latter being the 1963 March on Washington and Martin Luther King, Jr.'s, "I have a Dream" speech.

This was the ambience Mac Ireland was now soaking up like a sponge.

Anywhere outside the claustrophobic state of Northern Ireland, a Catholic feels himself breathing more easily. But for Mac Ireland, that feeling was magnified a thousand times. For him, the sense of freedom on The Mall was, at the same time, both stunning and exhilarating. No wonder Americans were big on freedom (strange, however, that many of them, therefore, did not understand the burning desire of the Irish for the same freedom and national self-determination). The openness, scope and expansiveness of The Mall were entirely splendid to him. How blessed Americans were.

Yet, he kept an eye on all the joggers and runners, wondering if Charlie Shepherd was among them. That soured the beauty of his walk and he shook himself out of it. I will leave all that until Sammy comes. I cannot do anything anyway. I just might as well enjoy the Nation's Capital. Later he planned to take in the famous museums of the Smithsonian Institution, the Capitol and the Library of Congress. Ah man, wouldn't Mary love all of this, he sighed.

CHAPTER 11

Sammy Johnson arrived two days later. Fr. Murphy welcomed him warmly and made him feel at home right away. "I knew your father and grandfather, Sammy. They were fine men, and would have made great Fenians," he joked.

Sammy laughed, "Just as Mac Ireland's father and grandfather would have made great Orangemen," he replied in kind.

The following morning Mac Ireland took Johnson for the two-hour walk on The National Mall. They mostly walked in silence.

They crossed over 7th Street and 14th Street keeping up a steady pace.

As they approached the Washington Monument, east of the Reflecting Pool and Lincoln Memorial, Mac Ireland paused and asked, "Sammy, how much do you know about The Monument?"

"Nothing at all. But I would be interested in finding out. What can you tell me?"

"It is constructed from marble, granite and sandstone. It is the world's tallest obelisk and the world's tallest stone structure – 555 feet and 5 .125 inches "(169.294175 meters). But here's what I wanted to tell you to gladden your Protestant heart." Then Mac Ireland put his left hand on Johnson's left shoulder, and pointing with his right hand said: "Look about 150 feet (46 m) up – about one-quarter's way up – The Monument. See where the different shading of the marble is?"

Johnson nodded.

Then Mac Ireland – with a grin as wide as Lough Erne or maybe the Potomac – chortled: "That's where some of your people blocked the construction of this magnificent monument for almost thirty years." And he threw back his head and laughed with delight.

"What do you mean my people?"

"Have you heard of the No Nothings?"

"No, I have not."

"They were an American nativist and anti-Catholic party in 1854 – a bit like the Orange Order and would have definitely contained some of your people."

Like lightening, Johnson jokingly punched him in the upper right arm.

Joking or not, Mac Ireland certainly felt it.

"Whoa, save it for the quare fella" (meaning, of course, Shepherd).

"Okay, now that I have stood up for my people, you may continue, you Fenian bastard," Johnson laughed.

"Well, as I was saying, before I was rudely interrupted by an Orange thump. ... Pope Pius IX, Pio Nuno, sent a 2000-year-old inscribed stone, acquired from the Temple of Concord in Rome, as his personal contribution to The Monument. The Orangemen – oops, sorry, the No Nothings – went berserk, interpreting this as proof that The Vatican was taking over America. They led a raid in the middle of the night, overpowered the Monument's watchman, stole the papal stone and dumped it in the Potomac, some say, or just smashed it, others claim. The next day, the Know Nothings took over the Monument Society. Chaos ensued, and Congress refused to appropriate any more money until the Know Nothings gave up control of the Monument Society in 1858 ... then, of course, the Civil War intervened, and the Monument was not finished until 1882."

"That's fascinating," broke in Johnson.

"But here's another thing that will also gladden your Protestant heart," added Mac Ireland.

"Oh, God, what now?" groaned Johnson in mock horror.

"You earlier used a common Unionist/Protestant/ Orange term, 'Fenian bastard.'" I call Pio Nuno the anti-Fenian bastard".

" Whoa, wait till I tell your Mother – you called the Pope a bastard – only my people do that," he guffawed. Why do you call him that?"

"Because he excommunicated the Fenians in 1870 – specifically declaring that not only the Fenians in Ireland but also the Fenians in America were excommunicated. And that four years after the Fenian Rising in 1867.

"He would have made a fine Orangeman," Johnson laughed.

"He was worse than a bigoted Orangeman – he was an Orange Tory and Monarchist. He was a disgrace to The Chair of Peter. How dare a Pope excommunicate Irishmen for fighting for the freedom of their country.

Had Pope Pius IX condemned the Fenians because he believed in the philosophy of non-violence that would have been a different matter? But that Pope did not believe in non-violence. He had his own Papal armed forces, and in 1860, he had appealed to Irishmen to come and fight for his stupid Papal States in Italy. About one thousand Irishmen – including Fenians – answered his call. So it was OK for Irishmen to fight for the Papal States, but it was a sin for them to fight for Ireland! That's the hypocrisy that drives me crazy."

"How do you know all this stuff, Patrick?"

"I am going to let you in on a secret, Sammy. We read. We Catholics read books," Mac Ireland grinned.

"Do you want another Orange thump, Mac Ireland?"

"No, no. As I said, "save that for the quare fella.""

Then Mac Ireland clapped his hands and smilingly said, "Well, that was a nice interlude, now let's continue".

After about one hundred yards, Mac Ireland asked the question they had so far avoided: "How are we going to do it?"

Johnson turned his head towards him, "For one thing, we cannot use guns (which we don't have anyway). If it is seen as an act of terrorism, we will have defeated our purpose, and we will not make it out of Washington alive."

This was a new game for Mac Ireland and he was content to let Johnson take the lead. With his background, Johnson knew the intelligence game far better. Operating on the Fermanagh-Cavan Mountains was second nature to Mac Ireland – The National Mall was something else.

Both men were wearing sunglasses and baseball caps. Mac Ireland in his wig was impossible to recognize. "Is there any danger, Sammy, that Charlie Shepherd would recognize you?" "Not at all. We've never met and he has no idea who I am. But, still, anytime I'm out in public, I will wear the sunglasses and baseball cap."

Mac Ireland nodded and then pointed to just northeast of the Lincoln Memorial. "Over there, Fr. Murphy tells me, there could be one day a memorial of the Vietnam War."

Sammy looked over, saying, "What a waste of lives."

"That's for sure. I just hope America does not start repeating all the mistakes of the British Empire."

Johnson glanced at him, suspecting it may have been another dig but then realized Mac Ireland was being serious and seemed lost in thought. So he did not respond in any way.

As they approached the Lincoln Memorial, Mac Ireland paused, "Sammy, before you get caught up in the grandeur of the Memorial, how are we going to get it done?"

Johnson faced him. "Remember, Patrick, I told you we would have to do it at close quarters – that you would not be able to do that. I have to take him down with a few punches, without any fuss or commotion, here on the National Mall where I have learned he runs. Then we have to dispose of the body when we've finished him off."

Mac Ireland immediately recalled how he and the two Cavan men had used a lake to take care of 'Middle Name" and he wondered if the Potomac could be used for the same reason. However, he didn't say anything.

As they climbed up the steep steps of the Lincoln Memorial, Johnson remarked, "I have to check a few things with my people. If Fr. Murphy lets me use his phone when we get back, I will be able to come up with something."

On the way back to the Monastery, both men kept an eye out for the running figure of Charlie Shepherd, though there was no sight of him.

Three hours later, Johnson taps on Mac Ireland's door and steps in. Mac Ireland, sitting on his chair by the small table, instantly knew something was up." Patrick, I've got something. Shepherd faithfully runs on the National Mall five times a week – Monday to Friday, inclusive. He starts out on 3rd Street St. SW at 6 AM and runs to The Lincoln Memorial and back again, arriving at 7 AM. Now for the bad news. He's being moved to the San Francisco Consulate in two weeks."

Mac Ireland rubbed his left hand over the top of his head down the back of his neck shoving it out to hold his left jaw as if he had a toothache. "Ah man," he whispered. And then rubbed the same hand down over his mouth, all the way to the bottom of his neck.

Johnson was standing up in the small room. "I was not expecting this. I was told he would be at the British Embassy for five years. I've no idea why he's being moved to San Francisco. We have to move fast – time is now against us. We have to take him down this coming Monday. ... This is Tuesday. ... That gives us almost a week. Unfortunately, Patrick, I've got to tell you the plan I originally had is not now possible."

"What was that plan?" asked Mac Ireland.

"I'm sorry, now I cannot divulge that."

Mac Ireland looked at him in exasperation. "What the hell, Sammy?"

"I cannot tell you, Patrick. I can only ask you to believe that, and trust me that I would not deceive you."

Mac Ireland held his head down for a long time.

Straightening up, he asked, "Okay, Sammy, okay. Now what do we do?"

Johnson held out his hands as if imploring, "I am hoping you can save the day. I have no Plan B."

Mac Ireland got up from his chair, "Alright, Sammy, head back to your room and I'll come by later."

CHAPTER 12

The moment Sammy left, Mac Ireland headed for Fr. Murphy's room. The priest was reading his Breviary as Mac Ireland walked in. "Fr. Terrence," Mac Ireland began, "We are going to need your help." Here we go, thought Fr. Murphy. I felt this was coming.

"Do you know the Cassidy brothers from Ballinamore, now living in New York – the cops who recently became detectives? Their grandfather fought the Black and Tans?"

"I do, indeed. They often come to visit me with a whole contingent of New York cops."

"Great, can you get them to come down on Sunday? Tell them to come in the largest detective car possible with that siren and all their fancy stuff. Tell them that I need their help. They know me. They are not to tell anyone else. Tell them to call me from a safe line so I can give them further instructions."

Mac Ireland hurried back to Johnson's room. As he entered, Johnson gave him his chair and sat on the side of the bed.

"I may have something, Sammy."

Johnson's eyes lit up.

"However," continued Mac Ireland, "needless to say,

you can never use any of this information in the future – no more than I can use yours, per our agreement."

"And I will honor it with my life just as I honor my son's memory," Johnson replied.

"Okay. Now tell me this: when you knock Shepherd out, can you finish him off, without making him bleed?"

"Yes, I had planned for that. I'll smother the bastard. There will be no bleeding – at least externally. What do you have in mind then?"

Mac Ireland leaned back in the straight backed chair to stretch out his legs full length and crossed his ankles and explained. "Two New York cops, detectives, are driving down to join us on Sunday. They will transport the dead body of Charlie Shepherd back to New York in their police car and dispose of it, in some way to be decided later when I talk to them. The moment we dump the body in the car, we head out of Washington immediately and go our separate ways."

Johnson leapt to his feet, throws out three punches and says, "Good man, Patrick. I think that can work."

That night the Cassidy brothers called Mac Ireland from a secure line.

"Hello Jack and Peter. I really need your help."

"You got it, Patrick. Just tell us what you want," assured Jack, the elder of the two by three years.

Jack had offered to come home and fight with Mac Ireland when The Troubles had erupted again. Mac Ireland had advised him he could serve the cause better in New York. Now he was glad he had. Peter was 34 and just as committed as his older brother.

"Boys, I am on the trail of the man who assassinated Fr. Maguire."

"Jaysus," the two brothers whispered simultaneously.

"Do you know who did it?" asked Jack.

"Yes, he's here in Washington."

"Do you want us to kill the bastard, Patrick?" Peter almost came through the phone.

"No, no, Peter. Another fellow and I are going to do that. But I need you to take his body back to New York and get rid of it somehow."

"Who's the other fella?" asked Jack.

"I'll fill you in on that when we meet. But boys, here's what we need. Come in one of those big fancy New York detective vans with sliding doors. We need to bundle Shepherd – that's his name – into the van, and then finish him off. There will be no blood or mess. The moment it's done, you have to get out of Washington, as do I. I'll see you on Sunday. Bring whatever will be useful – body bag, duct tape, etc."

"Don't worry, Patrick. We'll take care of it," promised Jack, as all three hung up.

CHAPTER 13

Mac Ireland and Johnson started their surveillance on Charlie Shepherd on Wednesday morning.

Johnson had brought two small, powerful binoculars. On their way over to 3rd Street S.W. at 5 A.M., he said: "Feel free using the binoculars. Nobody will regard it as unusual. They will think you are using them to get a better view of The Capitol. Let's split up a few blocks before we get to 3rd St. S.W."

Johnson went to the far side of the mall, Mac Ireland stayed on the Independence Avenue S.W. side of The Mall close by the Air and Space Museum. Mac Ireland explained he wanted to stay on that side of The Mall in order to spot Shepherd's left ear as he faced west to run toward the Lincoln Memorial

Sure enough at 6 A.M. on the dot, Charlie Shepherd appeared on The Mall at 3rd St. S.W. Mac Ireland focused his binoculars on him. Even without his bad ear, Mac Ireland would have recognized him. There was a certain cut to him. As Sammy's aunt predicted, "He's a man to be reckoned with."

As Shepherd did his stretches and limbered up, he moved like a big cat – a puma – with ease and strength. Mrs. Johnson had guessed he was a couple inches taller than himself. He was certainly that – Mac Ireland estimated. In fact, if anything, even more. He's at least six foot two, he noted to himself.

Then Shepherd took off on his run. At first, fairly slowly, then built up speed as he passed the Air and Space Museum.

Mac Ireland watched Shepherd race down The Mall, thinking, "I'm glad the hardy Protestant boy is with me. There is no way I could take this Brit by myself."

Mac Ireland followed the speeding Brit down The Mall. There was no danger of getting too close as Shepherd was already a quarter of a mile ahead.

Mac Ireland watched him through the binoculars, knowing Johnson, across The Mall, was doing the same. He saw Shepherd dash across 14th St., then pass the National Monument, which is about half way between The Capitol and the Lincoln Memorial and slightly west of center.

Mac Ireland made sure he would be nowhere near Shepherd's returning path – the gravel road that joggers and runners used right in the middle of The Mall from 14th St. to the Capitol. When Shepherd was returning, Mac Ireland was well off to the side, with his back turned, on Jefferson Drive, which runs right in front of the Smithsonian Institution Building, commonly referred to as The Castle. It was designed by James Renwick Jr., who also designed St. Patrick's Cathedral in New York. It is constructed of Maryland red sandstone in the faux Norman style ("a 12th-century combination of late Romanesque and early Gothic motifs"). It looks like a castle, and serves as the administrative offices and information center.

When Mac Ireland was sure Shepherd had left The Mall, he turned around and walked in the direction of the Lincoln Memorial knowing he would soon link up with Johnson again. He saw Johnson coming from the other side of 14th Street SW.

"So how did it go, Sammy?"

"I followed him all the way on the Constitution Avenue-side of The Mall. The boy can fairly move. It would be difficult for us to take him anywhere between 14th St. and the Lincoln Memorial."

"Don't worry, Sammy. I think I've got the best place to grab him. Let's head back toward the Capitol and I'll show you.

They strolled back and Mac Ireland surprised Johnson by stopping right in front of the statue of Joseph Henry opposite the entrance to The Castle.

Joseph Henry (1799-1878) was Scottish-American scientists whose father and mother were Scottish immigrants. He is acknowledged as the inventor of the electric motor and the father of daily weather forecasts. In his day, he was referred to as the, "Nestor of American science." (Nestor was the Greek mythological king who provided wise counsel and guidance).

He was First Secretary of the Smithsonian and shaped it into the institution it is today.

Yet, for all his eminence, this brilliant son of Scotland is barely known today. Indeed, the millions of people who pass his statue on The Mall each year hardly give it a second look – probably assuming it is a statue of English scientist James Smithson (1765- 1829), whose bequest in 1829 of about a half a million dollars provided the initial funding for the Smithsonian Institution.

The statue, built in 1883, is positioned 150 feet (45 m) from the northwest corner of the Castle. The pedestal – comprised of Maine red granite and Quincy (Massachusetts) grey granite is 4 feet (1.2192 m) in diameter and is 7'3" (2.2098 m) tall. The bronze statue itself is 9 feet (2. 7432 m). A total height of 16'3" (4.95300 meters). It depicts Henry in academic robes looking north, his left hand positioned on a book.

As Mac Ireland scrutinized the statue he was struck by the fact that Henry had died just one hundred years earlier – just a blip in Irish historical terms but half the age of United States.

Johnson's question pulled him out of his historical reflection. "But why here, Patrick? It seems too central."

"It is, but the statue does give us a little bit of cover from people who may be walking on Jefferson Avenue. And the police van will give us cover from those on The Mall. But we also need another car to lead the New York van and give it, so to speak, safe passage."

Johnson was silent and Mac Ireland realized that although his Protestant ally may have been proficient on intelligence matters, he was not too sharp on planning operations. Indeed, it was dawning on him that Johnson was so focused on getting his hands on his son's killer that he had not really given it much planning. He was still too deep in the grieving process to think strategically. His only "plan" – apart from having gleaned essential intelligence on the whereabouts of Shepherd – was to get close to the Brit killer and take him down with a few punches. We moved far too precipitously on this, Mac Ireland thought to himself, though that was all moot now. The die was cast. There was no going back.

If they called it off now, when would they get another chance? After all, he had to get back to fight the Brits on the Fermanagh-Cavan border, and God knows what Johnson had to do.

Both men stood and looked at the designated spot of their planned action as Joseph Henry impassively presided over them.

"Let's get back to the monastery. I've got to make some calls," Mac Ireland eventually suggested.

When they returned, Mac Ireland asked Fr. Murphy to get Jack Cassidy on the phone. He did, and left the room so Mac Ireland could speak in private.

"How's it going, Patrick?" asked Jack.

"Not too bad, Jack, but we will need a second car, also a police car. You and Peter will have to drive up the gravel path right in the middle of The Mall. D.C. police and utility vehicles do it. So it can be done. But it would be best if we could get a friendly police car to lead you and Peter. In that way, nobody would pay any attention."

"I've got the very man," Jack excitedly interjected. In fact, he's from your own county. His older brother was in the 1956 Campaign – Hugh Mc Caffery from the Roslea area.

"Sure, I know the family well. One of his young brothers went to America."

"That's the one I'm talking about. His name is Joe, and he is about 20 years younger than Hugh. He first came to New York. Then ended up in Maryland. And the next thing I heard, he was in the Capitol Police – the police who are in charge of the Capitol and The Mall. He's a sound man – IRA to the core. Nobody knows that except Peter and me. He has helped us before, and he will be honored to help Patrick Mac Ireland. He is well connected and will make the necessary arrangements to make sure nothing will go wrong".

"Ah, man, that's great, Jack. Set it up. Make arrangements for us all to meet up on Sunday evening at 8 P.M. Needless to say, do not meet in any other place. No, Irish bars, only in the monastery."

"You've got it, Patrick," Jack promised as he hung up.

Mac Ireland clapped his hands and whispered, "Man, this can now work."

He headed off to Johnson's room.

"Sammy, I think we've got it. A Capitol Police car will lead the New York police van onto the Mall. You and I will travel with the New York boys in their van. The Capitol police can park in front of the Joseph Henry statue, and the New York van will park facing the Capitol so the sliding door will face the Henry statue, not the open Mall. When the Capitol policeman sees Shepherd coming back on his run, he will call him aside, take him in between the New York van and the statue, and there you will be waiting to give him your best one-two – or three – if necessary. Then we dump him in the van. The Capitol police car escorts us out of town, as you finish Shepherd off. When it is done, we get out of the van, wave down a cab and go back to the monastery, and then out of town."

Johnson jumped to his feet and pumped Mac Ireland's hand. "As an Orangeman, it pains me to say this, but I'm beginning to understand why top British army specialists are saying they can never defeat you boys in the IRA."

"And you know what? They are right, too," grinned Mac Ireland.

Then he added, "Go ahead and make your arrangements for leaving Washington on Monday and I'll do the same. We don't need to know each other's arrangements. Also, on Thursday and Friday we will continue to monitor Shepherd's running."

CHAPTER 14

On Sunday evening, the Cassidy brothers and Joe Mc Caffery arrived. Fr. Murphy brought them along to meet Mac Ireland by himself, and then went back to his own office.

The three visitors were visibly excited to be in the presence of the legendary Mac Ireland. He welcomed them warmly and put them at their ease. After inquiring about their families, he filled them in on the progress of the Struggle back home.

"The Brits are not going to beat the IRA this time, boys. This time we're going to win."

That was greeted by smiles all around.

"Right now, however, we have to take out one of the most dangerous operators the Brits ever sent to The North. He has run agents at the top of the IRA. He personally assassinated Fr. Maguire as he knelt praying at the altar after saying Sunday Mass in Kincally. He killed Fr. Maguire because the priest had discovered one of the deadly British agents at the center of the IRA leadership. And if we don't take action, this murderous Brit will never be brought to justice."

Officer Mc Caffery jumped in, "Patrick, I haven't the slightest hesitation. I would never betray America or my duty as a policeman. Nonetheless, I have absolutely no duty to protect the oppressors of my country. And George Washington himself would agree with me as he always wanted Ireland to be free from England".

"Our sentiments exactly," chimed in Peter Cassidy.

"Good man, yourself, Joe. Now let me tell you about my accomplice. He's a Protestant originally from Kincally. He's an Orangeman."

He watched their feet shuffle.

"He's a policeman." The feet shuffling escalated.

"In fact, he's one of the top detectives in the North."

"Jaysus, Patrick, what hell?" blurted out Peter.

Mac Ireland was almost enjoying their consternation, but decided to quickly ease it. And he briefed them thoroughly on Sammy Johnson and on why they could trust him.

Then he brought Johnson into meet them. They exchanged pleasantries. Mac Ireland declared, "Sammy doesn't know anything about you, and he doesn't want to. It is not necessary for the mission. He just knows your first names. Now let's just go over some of the tactics and logistics for tomorrow. Then have an early night."

Later, Officer Mc Caffery went home to the outskirts of Capitol Hill and the Cassidy brothers stayed overnight in the monastery.

At 4:30 AM on Monday morning, Mac Ireland gave Johnson and the Cassidys a wake-up call. By 5 A.M., after a quick cup of coffee and some bread, they were out of the monastery and into the big fancy New York police van with its darkened windows. As arranged, they pulled up behind Mc Caffery's police car waiting outside The Voice of America building on the 300 block of Independence Avenue, S.W.

Just before 6 A.M., both cars drove up to 3rd Street. S.W.

Sure enough, the priest-killer Brit was doing his warm up exercises. They watched him take off on his run.

Then as arranged, they turned around, drove back to 4th Street, made a right, past the side of the Air and Space Museum, and after two hundred yards, turned a left, onto the gravel path in the middle of the Mall – the Capitol police car in the lead.

Mc Caffery had made arrangements that no other police cars would be on the Mall at that time.

With Shepherd well on his way, both cars slowly drove to the Joseph Henry statue. Officer Mc Caffery parked his car facing west toward the Lincoln Memorial. Jack Cassidy turned his van around, and parked parallel, between Mc Caffery's car and the statue – facing east, toward The Capitol.

Right on schedule – though it seemed to have passed more quickly – Shepherd was seen coming back, still running at great speed.

Officer Mc Caffery, resplendent in his Capitol police uniform, stepped into the middle of the gravel path, held up his hand – made sure there would be no trace of a Fermanagh accent.

"Excuse me, sir. An incident has been reported as happening on the Mall. You are one of the few out running this morning. Maybe you can help us."

"I'm British, Officer. I am attached to the British Embassy. I'm a strong believer in law and order. I'd be delighted to help," Shepherd volunteered in his almost stereotypically Eton-educated accent.

"Thank you, sir. Please come to the other side of our police van," and Officer Mc Caffery motioned for the obliging Brit to follow him. Then Mc Caffery stepped back, motioned with his left hand for Shepherd to move toward the open sliding door of the van, where Johnson was standing.

"Our detective will ask you the questions," Mc Caffery told Shepherd.

Shepherd gallantly strode forward toward Johnson. "How do you do, Detective. We Brits are happy to help the Washington police," and he held out his right hand. As he did, Johnson – picking the precise moment Shepherd would be at his least balanced – let loose with a thunderous right-hand haymaker of a punch.

Whether Shepherd sensed something or was just lucky, his head moved slightly down to the left. Johnson's fist caught him, not on the jaw, but higher up on the side of his head, thus lessening the blow. Still, it was a powerful punch and it spun Shepherd around to the right. Instead of going down, Shepherd, amazingly, continued to spin full circle, and ferociously, with his left foot, kicked Johnson on the right side of his jaw.

Mac Ireland had never seen the likes of it except in those martial arts films. As he jumped out of the van, he saw Johnson sag almost to his knees. Shepherd's left ear – that had caught the attention of Sammy's Aunt, Mrs. Johnson – was now in right in front of him. Mac Ireland punched the disfigured ear as hard as he could with his right fist putting his entire body weight behind it. He knew that would have put most men down, but it only staggered Shepherd. So he hit him again – two hard, short jabs.

Still, Shepherd did not go down but instead seemed to fully recover, turning on Mac Ireland with furious intensity.

"I'm finished now," Mac Ireland thought.

As Shepherd bore in for the kill, Sammy Johnson's fist exploded on his right jaw with a sickening thud.

Shepherd's knees buckled and as he turned to face his attacker, Johnson hit him in the solar plexus, knocking the wind right out of him. As he doubled over in excruciating pain, Johnson gave him a powerful left to the left jaw and caught him by the hair with his left hand before he went down. Then he jerked his head up and hit him with a devastating straight right.

Shepherd went straight up, straight back, and straight out for the count.

Johnson took time to catch his breath. He picked up Shepherd's feet; Mac Ireland picked up his shoulders, and they heaved him into the van.

"Let's go," shouted Mac Ireland.

The two vehicles took off, slowly without haste to 4th Street, made a left, then to the end of the Mall, and turned right – going up the Senate side of Capitol Hill on Constitution Avenue.

Johnson already had taped Shepherd's mouth with heavy duct tape, secured his hands, legs and feet with strong tape. Then he covered Shepherd's nose with a cloth soaked in chloroform supplied by the Cassidy brothers.

Next, he put the unconscious British-killer on the flat of his back on the bench seat in the back of the van, the head facing the passenger's side of the vehicle (not the driver's side, which in American vehicles is on the left).He instructed Mac Ireland to sit with all his weight on Shepherd's chest. Kneeling down, he put the heel of his left hand on Shepherd's forehead, slid his hand down, positioning it so he could clamp the nose firmly between his thumb and the side of the forefinger of his clenched fist. With his right hand, he pushed Shepherd's jaw up. There was no need to obstruct the flow of air into Shepherd's mouth, as the heavy tape had already sealed his mouth tight.

He patiently and clinically waited for the asphyxiation process to take its course – for the body's oxygen supply to be cut off. As he waited, Johnson thought he might later explain to Mac Ireland that the method they were using – simultaneous smothering and torso compression (sitting on the chest) – had been taught to him by the Brits. No one knew better than they how to restrain or torture, and if necessary kill a man, without leaving visible injuries. That prompted him to raise his head and glance at Mac Ireland. What he saw startled him: the intrepid guerilla fighter was squirming in revulsion, his eyes shut tight and his teeth clenched as if he were suffering more than the dying Shepherd. Clearly, this was not Mac Ireland's idea of fighting.

Johnson had been taught by the Brits that brain damage or even death can occur if a person is asphyxiated for over four minutes. He knew he had held Shepherd's nose for at least eight minutes. Because Shepherd's body had been weakened by the beating and the chloroform, he was sure he had finished him off. Still, he decided to wait another two minutes.

And just like that, it was all over. The most efficient killer the Brits had ever sent to The North lay lifeless. He would assassinate no more priests, handle no more traitorous agents in the IRA and cover up no more murders of young, innocent Protestant lads.

"Okay, men," Johnson instructed, "It's over. The bastard's dead."

Mac Ireland quickly got off the body in obvious relief, ashen face and visibly disturbed.

"Are you alright, Patrick?" asked Johnson.

Mac Ireland just nodded, keeping his head cast down.

"Patrick, you saved the day back at the Joseph Henry statue."

"We were lucky the Brit didn't finish the both of us," Mac Ireland softly answered.

Jack Cassidy shouted back, "Now men, change your clothing before you get out of the car. Leave your old clothing behind and we will burn it back in New York. He gave the signal – flashed head-beams twice and thumbs up out the window – to Officer Mc Caffery that he could now return to Capitol Hill. Then he pulled over and stopped the van.

Mac Ireland and Johnson quickly changed all their clothing, bid good-bye to the Cassidys, walked back on New York Avenue, and waved down a cab which took them to the monastery. The Cassidys proceeded to the Washington-Baltimore Parkway and then to 95 North back to New York. They were completely unperturbed by their lately departed "passenger," whose dead body they had placed in a large portable freezer in the back of the van.

Back at the monastery, Mac Ireland shook hands

with Johnson.

"Sammy, it was a victory for the Orange and the Green. We have far more in common than most people realize. If we could only get British injustice and sectarian politics out of the way – and a decent compromise – the Orange and the Green could live in peace."

"Amen to that," Johnson intoned, his right hand hurting as he pumped Mac Ireland's hand.

• • • • • •

Three weeks later, as Mac Ireland was safely back in Ireland, the news reported the astonishing story. The dead body of a British Embassy official was found in the QEII as its cargo was being unloaded in South Hampton, England.

That brought a smile to Mac Ireland's face. He had discussed the disappearance of Charlie Shepherd with the Cassidy brothers. Jack pointed out that some of the IRA supporters knew a certain organization in New York which was known to be able to bury bodies deep in cement hundreds of feet below the streets of the Big Apple. Jack also explained that IRA supporters on the waterfront and in the International Longshoremen's union (ILA) could safely dispatch the body back to England in the bowels of the QEII. Jack liked the irony of that. More importantly, he had explained to Mac Ireland, "By sending the body back to England, we will shift the focus of the police investigation out of the United States and into England. That is most important because Americans don't want to be associated with violence perpetrated on American soil." And then with a chortle he added, "And we can sweeten the deal by also shipping on the QEII a large consignment of weapons. Shepherd's body will be discovered – our weapons won't be."

Mac Ireland had approved the plan, and now three weeks later, he was pleased he had. He knew the British would play the whole thing down. It was not in their interest to have a full blown investigation as Shepherd's nefarious past would be aired in public – all the assassinations, the killing of Fr. Maguire, etc., etc.

However, Mac Ireland was conscious that it was important that the parish of Kincally would get closure and that they would be informed that Shepherd was Fr. Maguire's assassin, and that he had been brought to justice in the only possible way. Therefore, he had the word discretely passed around the countryside.

Meanwhile, Sammy Johnson had a headstone erected on his son's grave. "Oh Billy, I've done my duty and you can rest in peace." He prayed at the graveside. Well, not really prayed because Sammy wasn't sure he believed in prayer in the first place. Secondly, wasn't praying for the dead mostly a Catholic thing? "I must take that topic up with Mac Ireland if we ever meet again."

CHAPTER 15

Mac Ireland was surprised to get a message to call Fr. Murphy in Washington.

He was able to call the priest the following day.

Fr. Murphy wanted to know if he would give an interview to a reporter from The Washington Post if she were to travel to Ireland to interview him in person.

The priest added: "Washington media have had a hopeless record on Ireland. It just instinctively parrots British propaganda. The worst of all is Mary Mc Crory, who is supposed to be a big liberal and all for human rights. But on Northern Ireland, she's pathetic. She rants and raves about IRA violence, but never seriously takes on British institutionalized violence, torture of political prisoners and anti-Catholic discrimination, etc., etc. However, she is not entirely to blame. She takes her cue from the Irish Embassy, which seems to act as a wholly owned subsidiary of the British Government. Their only interest is in attacking the IRA and covering up for the Brits. Because you see, if the truth gets out about British violation of human rights, Americans will then be demanding to know why the Dublin government is doing nothing to protect the Catholics in The North."

Then Fr. Murphy explained that the young female

reporter, Emily Richardson, was fair minded and objective. She actually wanted to report the facts, not just regurgitate British propaganda, if *The Washington Post* would print it.

"Father, I'll meet her if she does not compromise my security. If she is prepared to accept the security arrangements my people make, then I'll give her an interview."

Twelve days later, Mac Ireland was sitting in a safe house being interviewed by the young woman from *The Washington Post*.

Reporter: "What are you fighting for, Mr. Mac Ireland?"

Mac Ireland: "For the same thing George Washington fought for – to kick England out."

Reporter: "But a million Protestants want England to stay."

Mac Ireland: "So did a lot of Americans during the American Revolution. It was your own John Adams, I believe, who memorably declared that a third supported England, a third supported the American Revolution, and the other third just didn't give a damn."

Reporter: "What about the use of violence?"

Mac Ireland: "Why is non-violence only preached to the poor and powerless, never to the rich and powerful? Why is it okay for an American to fight for his country, and a Brit for his, but not an Irishman? Why does America state it stands for national self-determination and international human rights, yet has 'a hands-off' policy when it comes to Northern Ireland?"

Reporter: "Why don't you try peaceful means?"

Mac Ireland: "We did for 800 years – apart from a few

isolated risings – 1798, 1803, 1848, 1867, 1916, 1919, 1956. Our latest peaceful attempt was the Civil Rights Campaign in 1968. The Brits beat the non-violent marches off the streets of Northern Ireland – and shot them down like dogs in Derry on Bloody Sunday, January 30, 1972."

Reporter: "Didn't the Cardinal of Ireland claim it was stupid to try and bomb a million Protestants into a United Ireland?"

Mac Ireland: "Well, with all due respect to the Cardinal, that was a stupid statement. Nobody is trying to do that. We are fighting to render English rule unworkable – to convince England its old game is up, and that Catholics never again will, 'go to the back of the bus'."

Furthermore, as regards the Cardinal. I like to quote the old saying: 'I take my religion from Rome but my politics from home.' I do not pay much mind to what the Hierarchy says about the fight for Irish freedom. The Bishops have always backed England, apart from a few honorable exceptions. Tis a miracle the Irish people remained Catholic. But it underscored that they had an informed faith – they knew the Church belonged to them and they were not going to let a few dozen pro -British Bishops steal it from them. They would keep their faith in spite of the Bishops. I would listen to the Cardinal if he, too, had taken to the streets in 1968 with the Civil Rights movement – had he gotten his head opened by the batons of the RUC and B-Specials like the rest of us, and had he gone to jail with the ordinary people. Do you think Martin Luther King Jr. would have had spiritual-moral authority had he stayed in the safety of the pulpit, too scared to put his body on the line? Would he have been in a position to preach non-violence to the poor, oppressed Blacks? Non-violent resistance (because that is what it is – resistance) can only be preached by those who practice it. The Cardinal does not practice it, ergo, he cannot preach it to others or me."

Reporter: "What would you settle for?"

Mac Ireland: "I'm not a politician. My job is to take the fight to the Brits, convince them they cannot beat us, and force them into talks. Nobody is demanding an outright British withdrawal. I know there has to be some sort of transitional period. I also accept that we have to reach an honorable compromise with the million Unionists. After all, partition has been a reality since 1920 and the Unionists/Protestants have been used to their own State. The fact that their leaders abused their power and oppressed Catholics (and were allowed to by the London) does not change the historical fact – they had their own State, and that has to be somehow taken into account. My fight has never been with my Protestant neighbors. My fight is against English rule and English oppression. England created an artificial state in the Six Counties in which sectarianism and anti-Catholicism were enshrined. England has violently maintained that state since 1920. I do not blame the Orangemen. I blame England."

Reporter: "But surely it was the Protestants, not the English, who were anti-Catholic. Aren't the English very non-sectarian?"

Mac Ireland: "Ah, The Big Lie, told successfully around the world. Imagine if there were a provision in the US Constitution forbidding an African-American being president, or forbidding the president to marry a black person. Wouldn't that have powerfully stoked the flames of racism and white supremacy? And wouldn't it be meaningless for Americans to deplore racism while leaving that provision intact?

Well as we speak – right now, not 200 years ago – there is a similar provision at the heart of the British Constitution.

The Act of Settlement 1701 is an integral part of the unwritten and uncodified British Constitution. It determines succession to the Crown of England, and is, therefore, a fundamental constitutional statute. Indeed, the very foundation stone of The Royal Family.

It contains provisions that decree a Catholic cannot succeed to the British throne and that if the Monarch becomes a Catholic, or marries a Catholic, he/she forfeits the Throne and 'the people are absolved from their allegiance.'

While this statute may mean little to the average Englishman in the street, it has always been of the utmost importance to Protestant/Unionist/Orange extremists in Northern Ireland. It provides the ideological and philosophical underpinnings for their bigotry and sectarianism. For you see, the spurious but deadly logic goes, if a Catholic by law can't get the top job, then Catholics are inferior to Protestants, and therefore it's okay to discriminate against them.

But don't first blame extreme Orangemen – they did not create the Act of Settlement.

Put the blame where it belongs: on the British Monarchy and Parliament – and on the Church of England and British Establishment for going along with this inherently sectarian constitution. (The constitution is also sexist and discriminates against women: If there is no direct male heir, a royal princess can succeed to the

Throne, but a younger brother takes precedence over an older sister.).

Now, Miss Richardson, I can see you were not quite aware of this – and you are a well-educated, modern woman.

I bet you, if there were a provision in the Irish constitution forbidding a Protestant being president, you would have heard of it. *The New York Times*, *The Washington Post*, etc. etc., would be regularly denouncing it and demanding its repeal. Why the double standard? Why the silence about the sectarian, anti-Catholic British Constitution? There is only one possible explanation: the media is desensitized on the rights of Irish Catholics – it is okay to discriminate against them.

Now if someone responds: "Doesn't the Queen have to be Protestant because she is the supreme head of the Church of England" … How does that answer anything? How can that be used to justify discrimination? Isn't that why the U.S. Founding Fathers in their wisdom kept Church and State separate: 'Congress shall make no law respecting an establishment of religion, or prohibiting the free exercise thereof...' because an Established Religion of its very nature institutionalizes discrimination?

Reporter: "Mr. Mac Ireland, you have been very generous with your time. May I conclude by asking you one final question: "What does the future hold for you?"

Mac Ireland: "God only knows. It will be a miracle if I survive. But I've made this pledge: I will continue the fight until Ireland is free."

Reporter: "Thank you, Mr. Mac Ireland."

CHAPTER 16

The leader of the SAS (Special Air Service) unit put his foot on Packie's neck, "One last time, where is Mac Ireland?"

"Go to hell."

The SAS killer removed his foot, leaned down and shot Packie in the middle of the forehead.

"Let's go," he ordered the three other men in his patrol, and then mockingly broke into song:

"Another martyr for old Ireland.

Another murder for the Crown."

The rest of the assassination squad laughed uproariously as they trekked across the mountain.

"Where did you learn the Kevin Barry song, Robert?" asked the one of the squad.

"My grandfather was Irish born. He had Irish pubs in Kilburn. He made his money from selling the Irish drink in London. I'm making my money by killing them in Belfast, South Armagh and Cavan." He had a self-satisfied chortle at his own cleverness. Then continued:

"As a boy, I was in his pubs occasionally, and I heard their stupid songs sung by those stupid Paddies. However, selling the Paddies drink left my own father well-off. He was able to send me to Ampleforth –

the Catholic college in North Yorkshire, run by the Benedictine Monks. You'd be surprised by the numbers of Catholics – well, nominal Catholics – that are in the British special services. A lot of us went to Ampleforth, where we were recruited. Though don't worry: we are more loyal than the most loyal English Protestants. And by the way, we are proud that the founder of the SAS, Colonel Sir David Stirling (1915 - 1990) was an old Amplefordian. Not only that, the founder of the Commandos, Brigadier Simon Fraser, 15th Lord Lovat (1911-1995), was also one of our "Old Boys." Now remember the general and useful distinction you were taught in training at the SAS headquarters in Hereford: commandos specialize in attacks on conventional military targets. The SAS specializes in counter-terrorism, intelligence and reconnaissance – and in what we just did to Packie. Yes, sir, the Benedictine Monks prepared us to reign down terror all over our empire. And now in the last little corner of our empire, Northern Ireland, you can count on Old Amplefordians doing their duty for Her Majesty's Government. Packie is only the first of Mac Ireland's team. We will get Mac Ireland and every fucking one of them – by any means necessary".

He led his squad of elite assassins off across the Border back into Fermanagh, where British Army and RUC vehicles picked them up.

The SAS patrol, having illegally crossed The Border, had caught Packie as he came out of a safe house near Ballyconnell. They had quickly overpowered him, knocked him unconscious and carried him off to the mountainside where they had killed him.

The British Government has never been too keen

to acknowledge they deployed the SAS in Northern Ireland, and, of course, they simply never would admit the SAS crossed into The Republic. The SAS were sent into The North in July 1970. Irrespective of how the rest of the world might see the SAS, in Ireland, they will always be viewed with opprobrium – the successors of the Black and Tans in ignominy.

Working closely with the British Army's Force Research Unit (FRU) – and with MI5 and MI6 – the SAS in Northern Ireland specialized in assassinations, kidnapping, dirty tricks, running agents/ double agents, and loyalist/Protestant death squads.

Historically, the SAS has an odious record in Aden (1963-1967), Oman (1958-59; 1970-76), Malaya (1950-59), Borneo (1962- 66).

Yet the British Establishment and a compliant media (including sections of the Irish media) have presented the SAS as dashing, romantic heroes – James Bonds in beige berets with winged-dagger badges. And that perfectly illustrates the difference between the English and the Irish view of history.

To the Irish, the SAS are elite assassins.

That, of course, may well be unfair to the individual members of the SAS, who may be decent guys. However, they do whatever Her Majesty's Government commands. It is well known that the British Cabinet has always had members who got their kicks from sending out their "derring-do boys " to teach Irish Catholics a lesson.

Nonetheless, it must be acknowledged that the SAS men do not lack courage. They are widely regarded as the most elite Special Force in the world – even superior, some claim, to the U.S. Navy Seals. Their motto is "Who Dares Wins."

Certainly, their selection and training are impressive. They famously train in the remote mountain range of the Brecon Beacons in South Wales. Pen y Fan is the highest point of the range: 2,906.82 feet (886m).

At the end of the first week, SAS candidates must do The Fan Dance: ascend the Pen y Fan and descend to the far side, then turn around and reverse the trek. In all, it's a march of 14.9 miles (48 km) and must be completed in four hours – while carrying a 40-pound backpack, rifle, and water bottle.

The final endurance test, known as The Long Drag, is a 40-mile (65 km) hike while carrying a 55-pound pack, which must be completed in twenty hours. All the more demanding because it comes at the end of four grueling weeks of marches and runs.

Only 10 out of 125 candidates make it.

Needless to say, the SAS are superior experts with all sorts of weapons. For their own personal guns, they once used the standard British rifle L1A1A SLR but soon replaced it with the M16. For their handgun, the Browning HP.

The SAS consists of three units, one Regular and two reserves – Territorial Army (TA).

The 22 SAS Regiment is the Regular Army Unit. It consists of four operational squadrons: A, B, D and G. Each squadron has a reported 60 men, divided into four troops, commanded by a major. It is believed that each troop has about 16 men, and each troop-patrol has four men. The Regiment is under the operational command of the Director of Special Forces (DSF), who is a major-general.

Kevin O'Neill broke the news of Packie's death to Mac Ireland. It was the bitterest of bitter news. Mac Ireland had known Packie since they were children running around the fields of the parish of Kincally, playing football, fishing and in general having great craic.

Attending Packie's funeral was out of the question for Mac Ireland. Indeed, one of the reasons Packie had been killed may have been to simply draw Mac Ireland out into the open.

Packie was buried in Kincally. Thousands of people flocked to his funeral. A lone piper led the funeral cortege from the church to the graveyard. The coffin was draped in the Tricolor and surrounded by a color guard – four men and four women on either side, dressed in black clothes and wearing black berets and dark sunglasses.

Rows and rows of strong local farmers encircled the color guard making sure the Brits and RUC couldn't send in "snatch squads" to grab the IRA volunteers. Irrespective of what those people may have felt about the IRA, there was no way they would allow the Brits or the hated RUC to invade the sacredness of the graveyard to grab the young Volunteers who were risking their liberty to honor their fallen comrade.

The priest finished the funeral prayers and departed. Immediately hundreds of umbrellas were raised as if by magic, and held high. Then they were taken down, and three masked men stepped forward and fired a volley of shots. The umbrellas were raised again and taken down when the masked men had been spirited away, having done their duty to Packie. Slowly the crowd dispersed, many muttering imprecations against the assassins of its SAS.

On the top of the hundreds of wreaths that lay around Packie's grave, was one that stood out: "Your death has not been in vain. – Your comrade, Patrick Mac Ireland."

Shortly after Package's funeral, Mac Ireland traveled with Kevin into Leitrim to meet with the Army council of the IRA – the seven member council that ran the organization on a day to day basis. The men were from Cork, Dublin, Belfast, South Armagh, Derry and Belfast.

Mac Ireland knew them all, some of them for many years. He noticed with particular interest that none of them mentioned Emmet Mulligan or "Middle Name."

Mac Ireland made his pitch quickly and to the point: "My team, Flying Column as I still call it, is under attack. The Brits are out to destroy us. Kevin and I are here to request your total support. We can do the fighting, but we need more semtex, more guns and more money. We need to hit back with unprecedented ferocity. Give us more SAMs and not British helicopter will fly anywhere in South Fermanagh.'

Kevin O'Neill chipped in, fuming: "Our comrade Packie was gunned down within the Free State. The Free States make it difficult for our men and women to move around. Yet, the SAS were able to come into County Cavan and assassinate Packie. And the useless Dublin Government will not say a word."

There was a murmur of assent from the Army Council. But Mac Ireland couldn't help wondering which of its seven members were working for that very Dublin Government – not to mention the London Government.

Anyway, the Army Council pledged full logistical

and materiel support.

On the way back to Cavan, and about half an hour after the meeting, Kevin O'Neill asked, "Patrick, do you think we can trust all of them boys?"

When Mac Ireland did not answer, Kevin, who was driving, turned and looked at him, making it clear he expected an answer.

"Kevin, you are a countryman like myself. I think we have to use all our country cunning. We are in a deadly dangerous time. We have to be extremely careful".

'But, do you trust..."

Before he could finish his sentence, the windscreen exploded and half of Kevin's head was blown away.

"Oh, Christ, Kevin," Mac Ireland yelled as he saw Kevin's head explode, and the car head for the ditch. Mac Ireland frantically grabbed the wheel and managed to steer the car so that instead of crashing head on, it scraped the side of the ditch, deeper and deeper, until it was forced to stop – still on the proper, left side, of the road.

Mac Ireland grabbed Kevin, but it was obvious that the stalwart young Tyrone man was already dead.

As Mac Ireland tried to figure out where the shots had come from, he heard the sound of screeching tires. He looked around and saw a car careening toward him. He then realized that the car that he had seen coming toward them a few seconds earlier was where the shots had come from, and now it had reversed and was coming back to finish the job.

Mac Ireland jumped out of the car and scrambled up on the side of the ditch. As he reached the top, two shots caught him square in the back. He pitched forward falling down through the hedge to the other side.

As the car came to a halt, the shooter jumped out to follow his prey, but then a tourist bus came from behind and blew its horn loudly and persistently. At the same time two cars came from the other direction.

"Into the car," screamed the British accent of the driver. The dark clad gunman paused, looked at the driver as if undecided what to do. "Into the fucking car, NOW," the driver ordered.

The bus loaded with tourists, some with heads out the windows, sounded its horn again. The gunman reluctantly got back into the car which screamed off with ferocious speed.

By now the first oncoming car had stopped, and the driver had gotten out to inspect the crashed car Kevin O'Neill had been driving. "He's dead, he's dead," the motorist shrieked, and stood in front of the bus forcing it to come to a halt. "Get help, get help," he cried out.

Tourists rushed off the bus to gawk. "That man has been shot," someone yelled. Pandemonium ensued.

On the other side of the ditch – unbeknownst to everyone in the excited crowd on the road – Mac Ireland's prone body began to stir.

"Oh God, what's happened?" Mac Ireland whispered to himself. "Where am I?"

And suddenly, in a flash, he knew exactly what had happened. "Thank God I was wearing my bullet-proof vest."

Mary had asked him to promise her that he would always wear it. He hated the bloody thing, though from now on, he would use "blessed" instead of "bloody" when thinking of it.

He peeped through the edge, saw all the commotion, and knew he had to get out of there. There was nothing he could do to help poor Kevin, and if the Guards on the Special Branch caught him, there could be endless difficulties. If nothing else, he could be put away for years, or if any of the Special Branch were in the pay of the British, he would get a bullet in the back of the head.

His first reaction was to keep heading on foot over the fields. But his chest was hurting and he feared some of his ribs could have been broken. He felt winded and a bit dizzy.

Then he heard the bus driver shout, "Ladies and Gentleman, please back on the bus. We must be in Cavan town in one hour."

Mac Ireland quickly figured this was his best chance. He made sure his wig was straight, dusted himself off, walked further down the inside of the hedge, and exited behind the bus. The bus driver was still pleading with the tourist to get back on board. Mac Ireland smartly boarded the bus, walked half way down where an elderly lady was sitting by herself.

"Someone has taken my seat. Is it okay for me to sit beside you, Missus?" he asked politely. The lady nodded.

The bus took off. Mac Ireland closed his eyes and prayed for the soul of his trusted second-in-command.

"They got Packie and now they've got Kevin," he silently grieved.

The pain in his chest had subsided. He put his head back and willed himself to go to sleep. He woke up as the bus pulled up in front of a hotel. Mac Ireland moved with the flow of the disembarking passengers and within minutes was on his way to a safe house.

As he entered the middle-aged woman of the house almost yelled, "Oh my God, Patrick. We feared you had been killed. We got a message saying you were in the car with Kevin. Oh my God. Oh my God."

"It's okay, Maggie, it's okay."

The woman's husband came in from the back yard.

"Lord, what happened, Patrick?"

Mac Ireland filled him in. And then requested, "Jim, help me off with this bullet proof vest, please."

Between the two of them, they got the vest off. Studded neatly in the back of the vest were two bullets.

"Oh, Mother of God. Jesus, Mary and Joseph. You could have been killed, Patrick," Maggie shrieked.

"I guess that was the idea, Maggie," he grinned. And then winced from pain in his chest.

"Oh God, he has been shot," cried Maggie. Patrick looked at Jim and assured him the bullets have not penetrated the vest.

"Now, Maggie," Jim pleaded, "don't fret. He's alright."

"I'm going to make sure. I'm going to get Dr. Quinn. And she was out the door to get the local doctor whom they knew could be trusted.

"Sit down, Patrick, sit down. What are we to do?"

"Jim, they probably think I'm dead. They saw me taking two slugs in the back, so it's best if I continue to let them think I'm dead. If the bus and cars had not come along, I certainly would have been finished off." When the doctor has checked me out, you drop me off and don't say anything to a soul until I get back to you. All our lives are on the line now, and we must be extra careful."

The doctor arrived quite quickly. Checked Mac Ireland out. Didn't think any ribs were broken, just bruised. Told him to take it easy for a while – "As if you are going to listen to that advice," he dryly deadpanned.

When Mac Ireland had been dropped off, he made his way to Mary's home. He needed to speak to her before anyone else did. Mary was surprised, yet thrilled, to see him.

He filled her in as she listened in stunned silence.

"Mary, I don't think it is safe for you to be living at home anymore."

"I'm not leaving, Patrick."

"Mary, listen, they're out to kill me. It's possible they know you are my wife. And if they know that, then you are in danger. They will kill you or have one of the Protestant paramilitary groups kill you."

"Patrick, I'm not scared."

"Well, I am, Mary. You must listen to me, please. You must trust that I know what I'm talking about. If you are not safe, then I won't be either.

That seemed to focus her mind, and she nodded gently.

"Mary, Sweetheart, you've been saying that you would like to go back and visit the family in France whom you stayed with when you were studying the language there. Why don't you do that for a couple of months until things cool off? I could even go there and see you. It would be easier going there than any place in Ireland. Do this, please, for me. We both will be safer if you do. You will be out of harm's way, and I can concentrate on what I have to do."

Mary got up and hugged him. "Okay, Love, I'll

do it. I have a lot of leave coming and I can head off tomorrow."

He kissed her, held her tightly. "God bless. I love you. I have to go. I'll call you in France.

And he was off into the Cavan night.

He headed for his ultra-secret dugout – the one where he did his best thinking and that nobody knew existed.

CHAPTER 17

Sammy Johnson found himself thinking a lot about Mac Ireland since their sojourn in Washington. His aunt in Kincally, Mrs. Johnson, was quite right. Mac Ireland was an unusually fine man: "Isn't it ironic that I should end up thinking Mac Ireland is the most impressive man I've ever met, and him a Fenian, standing for everything I oppose."

As he ruminated on the ironies of The Troubles with all its contradictions, conflicts and tragedies, his secretary in the outer office knocked on his door. "Sir, you have a call from a family member in Fermanagh.

Sammy picked up the phone.

"Sammy, it's your cousin Bobby in Kincally. I've had bad news. Aunt Vera was murdered. I found her body when I called to see her this morning."

Sammy groaned in agony. His dear wife had died young from cancer, his son Billy was taken from him... and now, Aunt Vera – the last of his father's brothers and sisters.

"What happened, Bobby?" asked Sammy.

"I don't know. The RUC are here at the moment. They have the whole place blocked off. I called them about thirty minutes ago."

"Bobby, please tell me the details – where was she shot, where did you find her, etc."

"Okay, Sammy. When she didn't answer the door, I used the key she had given me. She wasn't downstairs so I went up and knocked on her bedroom door. No answer, so I walked in. She was lying face down with half her head missing, covered in blood. It seemed as if she were dead for hours as her arms were totally cold."

Sammy listened in horror already assigning blame in his head.

"Sammy, who do you think did this? Do you think it was the Catholics or IRA?"

"Absolutely not," Sammy snapped. "You must spread the word immediately that this was no Catholic tit for tat thing. It was not done in retaliation for Fr. Maguire's murder."

"Okay, Sammy, though I should mention I heard several of the RUC men say it was done in retaliation."

"Listen to me, Bobby. The Catholics didn't kill Aunt Vera. Never mind what the RUC says. Look, I'm going to get ready to leave for Fermanagh. I will see you in a few hours in Aunt Vera's."

When Johnson arrived at his Aunt Vera's, he found the RUC gone, and the house full of local Protestants, and quite a number of Catholics. None of them would have known he was a detective. He had rarely gone back in recent years – ironically because Mac Ireland had made the area unsafe for policemen.

Not one person indicated they felt the murder was done by Catholics. It was amazing how country people had their own "local intelligence" system. They always knew what was what. Just like the Catholics knew immediately that Fr. Maguire's murder was not the actions of some Orange fanatic. Somehow country folk could just sense these things.

Furthermore, Kincally was never a sectarian cockpit – like Belfast or Portadown. There had never been a real sectarian atrocity in the area.

Johnson stayed for several days with his cousins. After the funeral, he requested some time off, and headed for Dublin. He was going to have to make contact with Mac Ireland, far earlier than he ever guessed he would. Indeed, he had taken for granted he would most likely never see Mac Ireland again.

He guessed Mac Ireland was probably only a few miles away over the Border, but he knew it would be crazy to try and meet him there. The anonymity of Dublin was necessary for such a meeting.

Mac Ireland had given him a secret number to call – on condition it was strictly related to their previous "joint venture."

"Just ask for 'The Fisherman' at that number," Mac Ireland had explained, "and he can get a message to me."

Johnson borrowed a car from his cousin Bobby, leaving his own in a hayshed on Bobby's farm. It was best not to travel in his own car over The Border.

He decided this time to stay in one of the loud, busy hotels near the airport, and just wait to hear from Mac Ireland.

As it happened, he heard from Mac Ireland rather quickly. Mac Ireland had been in Dublin himself meeting with the Army Council, briefing them on the Kevin O'Neill shooting. He was about to head back to the Fermanagh Border when The Fisherman got the message to him.

Mac Ireland rapped on Johnson's door on the third floor.

"Come in, Patrick."

When Mac Ireland stepped into the room, Johnson noticed he was about seven pounds lighter and looked a bit haggard.

"Sammy, I'm deeply sorry about your Aunt Vera."

"Thanks, Patrick."

The two men sat down somberly and wearily at the small table in the room.

"So, now, Patrick, the Brits are killing priests and old Protestant women."

"Sammy, they've always had a history of killing priests. God rest your poor Aunt. She was a lovely lady and didn't deserve this. I feared it might happen. I warned her that even though she was a Protestant, them boys wouldn't hesitate to kill her."

Then he paused, looked steadily at Johnson, "Where does all this leave us, Sammy?" Johnson groaned deeply, and leaned back and looked up to the ceiling.

"I'm not sure. We have to figure out who knows what. Do they know about us and Shepherd? Will the guy or guys who killed Aunt Vera be coming after you and me?"

"Oh, they've already came after me," laughed Mac Ireland. And he then explained he was in the car with Kevin O'Neill when he was shot.

"Oh my God, I wasn't aware of that."

"Oh yes, they think I'm dead, and I would have been had it not been for my bullet proof vest. I got away from the scene without being identified. So, Sammy, while you may have outed one British agent in the IRA – that bastard Mulligan – you clearly left another one untouched. "

"Not intentionally, I assure you."

"I know, Sammy, I know. I didn't mean to imply you had misled me."

"Alright, no harm done, Patrick. Now here's the thing we've got to figure out. Was my aunt executed because she saw Shepherd running away from the church? Or, was she killed because she was my aunt?"

"Maybe both."

"However, I don't think they could have figured out I was involved in what happened in Washington."

"Sammy, maybe it doesn't matter in one way. Maybe we are wasting our time trying to figure it out. Look, they came after me. Admittedly, they didn't need a particular reason for that. Still, the fact is that they also, around the same time, went after your aunt. Irrespective of what they know about you, I take it you are here because you want to bring the killer of your aunt to justice – just as you brought Shepherd to justice?"

"I see," responded Johnson.

"Sammy, we are not going to be able to figure much out at this meeting. You are going to have to go to Belfast, snoop around, analyze if the police report reveals anything, and then we should meet again."

"Yes, but let me ask you, Patrick, do you think that you and Kevin O'Neill were set up by someone in the IRA?"

"Yes, I most certainly do. Nobody knew about our trip into Leitrim except top members of the IRA," (He did not offer the information that he had been meeting with the IRA Army Council.).

"We must assume," Mac Ireland continued, "that the other spy at the head of the IRA is also being handled by the same person who assassinated your aunt...and that it is just a matter of time before he comes after you.... Therefore, once again, it is in our mutual interests to work together without either of us betraying his core principles."

"Whoever would have imagined it would come to this?" smiled Johnson. Then he became serious again.

"Patrick, can I ask you this before you go? You know, I'm still grieving deeply for my son Billy. I put up a headstone to him recently and as I stood at the grave, I found myself wanting to pray for Billy. Then I wasn't sure if I believed in prayer, and finally, I wondered if it's only something Catholics do – that is, pray for the dead. What do you think? I know you have seen a lot of suffering and grieving."

"My goodness, I didn't see that coming, Sammy. At any rate, let me take a shot at it – no pun intended. The Catholic Church may have messed up on a number of things. But we got the theology of death right – prescinding from the nonsense of Limbo. We believe it is, indeed, a "holy and wholesome thought to pray for the dead that they may have remission for their sins." All Christians believed that up until the Reformation and that quote is from the Bible, the Second Book of Maccabees. Luther didn't like that verse because it didn't agree with his new teaching. Therefore, the two books of Maccabees were excised from the Protestant version of the Bible. That was a great pity because it is the most natural thing in the world to pray for a deceased family member. In fact, it is so natural that we would have to deliberately stop ourselves from doing it. What could be more natural and loving for a son to say, 'God rest my Mother,' or for a father to say, 'God rest my son, Billy?'"

With that, Johnson broke down crying. He sobbed uncontrollably, great heaves of grief erupting from deep within his heart and soul.

Mac Ireland – well used to people grieving – wasn't the slightest uncomfortable. He sat in easy silence. Then he urged, "That's alright, Sammy. Let it all out. It's exactly what any loving father does. Let it all out."

And he sat again in silence as Sammy cried his heart out.

After about fifteen minutes, Mac Ireland explained, "Sammy, the only way I know of dealing with great suffering is to cry your eyes out, and pray your heart out."

After another prolonged period, Sammy composed himself. "Sorry about that, Patrick, and thanks for your help."

"Never feel embarrassed for crying and grieving, Sammy. I've sat up whole nights with some of the toughest men in Ireland while they cried their eyes out over the death of family members.

And, Sammy, let me add this – praying for loved ones makes sense irrespective of what one thinks of the doctrine on Purgatory. Look, all Christians believe that we are baptized into the mystical Body of Christ. We are members of His body. We form a communion in Christ, which cannot be broken by death. We Catholics call it the, 'Communion of Saints.' It makes complete sense… So pray for Billy, and ask him to pray for you, as he is now in the presence of God."

Then he jumped to his feet. "I've got to go. The Fisherman will always be able to reach me. Watch yourself and God bless."

And he was gone into the Dublin night.

CHAPTER 18

A few days after Mac Ireland had returned to the Fermanagh-Cavan Border, he got a message that Kevin O'Neill's younger brother Liam wanted to see him. Mac Ireland knew that Liam – three years younger than Kevin – was an active IRA member in East Tyrone.

When they met at a forest near Ballinamore, Liam got right to the point. "Patrick, my unit gave me permission to do this – I want to take Kevin's place. I can do for you everything he did. I am proficient with guns, explosives, and SAMs. Indeed, Kevin always told me I was as well trained as he was, and maybe even better as I've been in the IRA longer."

Mac Ireland grabbed his hand.

"Any brother of Kevin O'Neill is good enough for me. Kevin was a splendid man and one of the best IRA soldiers I've ever seen. We will be proud to have you in our Flying Column. I realize most don't use that term anymore, nonetheless, I like to hold on to it. It connects us with the 1956 Campaign and with all its predecessors."

Liam stood up and pumped Mac Ireland's hand.

"Just one thing, Liam. I understand you want to get justice for Kevin. But you must not allow emotion to cloud your judgment. That will not get justice for Kevin, but will get us all killed."

Liam nodded and assured Mac Ireland that he understood that perfectly.

Then Mac Ireland suggested, "You will want to hear about Kevin's last hours. Let's stroll up the side of this forest. It is quite safe at night right now."

Liam had the same cut about him as Kevin had. Confident in his walk and speech, he was a little smaller than Kevin but just as hardy. He radiated a quiet authority just like his hero-brother. Liam had been a law student at Queen's University but put his studies on hold to dedicate himself full time to The Cause.

The following night Mac Ireland had his team assemble in a safe house that they had never used before.

He introduced Liam O'Neill and explained he would be taking Kevin's place. The other men were relieved at that because they knew none of them could fill Kevin's shoes.

Then Mac Ireland added, "I've found a replacement for Packie, God rest him. He is Jimmy Mc Govern who knows the area well. You will meet him soon. But right now, let me fill you in on an operation Kevin and I had been planning.

One of my uncles always claimed that Kincally barracks could be 'taken out.' I think he was right, and Kevin felt it could be done. Liam, here, is skilled in the use of SAMS. The rest of you are familiar with semtex, of which we have an abundance. I've made arrangements to have a dozen SAMS delivered to our Column, and we have more than enough AK-47s and Armalites. We will be joined by ten experienced men from South Armagh.

After we take out the barracks, we are going to draw the British Army right to the border where the Mullan Customs Post was blown up several times during the 56 IRA Campaign. We will have the entire area rigged with semtex. Don't worry; there will be no civilian causalities. All the roads will be blocked off. Half the people in Kinawley are now primed to help because the Brits killed Fr. Maguire, and poor Mrs. Johnson.

Men, this could be the biggest body blow we ever gave the Brits in this part of Ireland. We are going to pick a day when no police are in the barracks – all the better to show the world that our fight is against The British Crown, not Ulster Protestants."

Two weeks later, everything was in place. Mac Ireland had organized it down to the last detail. Liam O'Neill had been shown the lay of the land. The fierce boys from South Armagh were gradually making their separate ways into the Cavan side of the Border. And they came armed to the teeth. "Ah, boys," Mac Ireland explained, "we have enough guns for all of you."

"We always bring our own," grinned their leader.

"Never leave home without them," joked another.

These are hardy boys, Mac Ireland thought to himself.

The evening of the planned operation, the village of Kincally was empty. The villagers were all attending a concert in a neighboring parish hall about five miles away, but still inside The North.

As it was getting dark, a large tractor with a huge trailer approached the barracks.

"Slow down, mate, watch the ramps," the British sentry on duty helpfully shouted out.

The driver, Jimmy McGovern, politely grinned beneath his large cap and waved to acknowledge the helpful advice.

The tractor, as instructed, moved slowly across the speed ramps. But as had happened before, with other tractors whose trailers had not been properly secured, the trailer appeared to bounce up and disconnect from the tractor.

"Hey, Paddy, your trailer has come off," shouted the soldier, as if it were an everyday occurrence.

Jimmy McGovern kept driving for about a hundred yards then jumped off the tractor. He waved to the soldier signaling that he understood and shouted, "Just a minute, Sir," and acted as if he was going to get a tool from the other side of the tractor. But, instead, once on the other side of the tractor, he walked quickly to a waiting car with Mac Ireland sitting in the passenger seat, Liam O'Neill in the back and Eammon in the driver's seat.

"Okay, let's go," directed Mac Ireland.

The car drove toward the border and stopped after a few hundred yards.

"Alright, boys. You know what you have to do once I hit the remote control and detonate the bomb."

The three got out of the car from where they had a safe view of the barracks.

"Okay, boys, here it goes," and he pressed the detonator.

The one thousand semtex bomb went off with such force that it almost knocked the three of them off their feet. The entire Kincally area was lit up with a blinding light. The barracks erupted as it were a house of cards. Cement blocks, British soldiers, barbed wire, flood lights, high towers, iron gates – all the symbols of British rule in Kincally – were spewed into the air with extraordinary velocity.

Even Mac Ireland and his two men were stunned by the fearsome destruction taking place before their eyes.

When things had subsided a bit, Mac Ireland directed, "Okay, Liam, let it rip." And Liam unleashed the SAM, which was the signal for the South Armagh boys who had taken up position on a hill overlooking the rear of the barracks. They contributed five more SAMS to the smoldering ruins of the barracks and the surrounding fortress that was above the ground. Also, they knew they had to watch for the responding counter attack coming from the Brits who would emerge from the huge underground structures.

In short order, dozens of British soldiers emerged from underground – thinking it was simply only a bombing attack.

Then the South Armagh boys demonstrated why they were the most feared fighters the IRA ever produced. They subjected the Brits to a withering reign of fire – sending the Brits scattering and about six of them down.

Liam O'Neill opened up with two more SAMS. And for good measure, Jimmy Mc Govern let loose with his Barrack Buster – a crude but deadly effective homemade mortar.

The barrack buster was the signal for all the IRA men to disengage and make it back to the base. "Look out for the helicopters," Mac Ireland had warned them.

Mac Ireland   directed the other two to get into the car and they took off. After a mile and a half, they abandoned the car where the road was, according to the plan, entirely blocked by two large tractors as were all the surrounding roads blocked by similar obstacles.

The three men with Eamon, the driver, jumped out of the car and quickly trekked across the fields, and crossed the Border. They took up their positions with four other men who were waiting there.

Mac Ireland knew the British soldiers and the RUC would head for the Mullan Border crossing. He had watched them do that many times.

Once the Brits had cleared off all the roadblocks, six truckloads of them made their approach to the Mullan border crossing. Within seconds, the inevitable helicopter appeared.

Mac Ireland had instructed his men that the helicopter had to be taken down first; otherwise it would disappear at the first sign of danger.

The soldiers on the ground were obviously waiting for instructions from the helicopter that it was safe to get out of their vehicles and take-up their positions to the left of the road. Mac Ireland whispered to Liam, "They're all out now. The moment you fire the SAM. I set off the semtex."

O'Neill took long, easy breaths: "This for you, Kevin." And he unleashed the deadly missile. Simultaneously, Mac Ireland pressed the remote control, and whispered, "And this is for Fr. Maguire, Mrs. Johnson and Packie."

Again, the Kincally area had never witnessed such a blinding conflagration in the Fermanagh skies. The helicopter disintegrated in an absolute inferno of death and destruction. Almost simultaneously, the 1,000-pound Semtex bomb erupted with volcanic intensity and merciless fury. Vehicles, bodies, guns, boots, clothing, eyeglasses, caps, and all sorts of debris, were spewed into the night air.

Amid shrieks and curses, the remaining soldiers ran to the right side of the road to take cover behind a large stone wall. It was a deadly mistake. Mac Ireland had stationed fifteen men from the Leitrim IRA on a hill with a perfect view of the wall. They opened up with their AK47s and Armalites. Within minutes, not one body by the stone wall was moving. It was all over

Mac Ireland fired one shot into the air from his Browning HP – the signal for all to disengage.

The following morning, the radio and press reported the terrible carnage: 24 soldiers killed in the destruction of Kincally barracks, 13 seriously wounded and 10 survived without injury.

At the Border Crossing, 27 British soldiers killed. No survivors.

The politicians went into frenzy. The Dublin Government warned there would be no safe haven for the IRA. The British Government hinted it might consider erecting a high wall along the entire length of the Border. The churchmen deplored the violence.

But all over Ireland – North and South – ordinary men and women were raising their glasses to toast Mac Ireland and his men.

Mac Ireland himself wasted no time in disappearing from the Border, and he had directed everyone involved to do the same. In a matter of hours, he was in a safe house just outside Virginia. He knew the news would be flashed all over the world, and that Mary would hear about it. So, he got a message to her that he was alright, and that he would call her in a few days.

In the morning, Mac Ireland was driven – in a relay of different cars – to Dublin where he had arranged for Liam O'Neill to link up with him.

They met in a safe house in Blanchardstown. "Liam, Kevin would be proud of you. You struck an important blow for freedom."

"And all of Ireland is proud of you, Patrick. It was an historic victory."

"Yes, Kevin – sorry, Liam, I keep calling you Kevin – though we must remember that for every action, there is an opposite and equal reaction. The Brits will be out for blood now. You must be extremely careful.'

Then he grabbed Liam by the forearm. "Liam, I have to tell you this. Your brother Kevin is dead because there is still another British agent at the head of the IRA. That agent set up Kevin and me for assassination."

"I've always suspected that. My unit in Tyrone always believed there were agents at the top of the IRA and Sinn Fein."

"Liam, I can't go into all the details yet, but I think I can uncover the agent. I need you to take care of things in my absence; I won't be able to get the job done if I remain around the Fermanagh Border. Also, it would be foolish for me to be there. They could get me too easily. Keep your head down. Do not say anything to any member of the Army Council or, indeed, to any of your men. We are in most dangerous times now, Liam".

Liam nodded soberly. "You can count on me, Patrick. I will be as loyal as my big brother. Go with God. Take care."

Mac Ireland was picked up by two middle-aged women and driven into the Dublin City center. He dropped into a shop on Grafton Street, nodded to the owner who took him into a back room. "There's the phone, Patrick. Take all the time you need. When you are ready to leave, I will have someone drive you."

Mac Ireland sat by the phone dialed and was soon talking to his secret wife.

"Oh, Patrick, how are you?" Mary cooed into the phone.

"And, Sweetheart, how are you?"

When Mary was assured he was okay, she told him all about France and the lovely family she was staying with. Mac Ireland promised her he would go to her soon.

They spoke for close to an hour before hanging up.

Mac Ireland had arranged for one of his supporters to book a room in a busy hotel, check in, and then hand over the room to him. He went to the lobby of a swanky hotel near Grafton Street, and called the emergency number to get a message to reach Sammy Johnson.

"Did you come up with anything, Sammy?"

"Yes, I did. We should meet." And then added slyly, "I see you've been busy."

Mac Ireland gave him the address of the hotel, and Sammy promised he would see him tomorrow evening.

CHAPTER 19

This time it was Mac Ireland's turn to tell Johnson to enter.

"Come in, Sammy."

They quickly shook hands.

"No trouble getting out of The North?"

"No, Patrick. Of course, I can't be certain that they don't have me under surveillance. I had to be really careful accessing the confidential information."

"Sammy, what have you got?"

"They guy who killed Kevin O'Neill is the same guy who killed my Aunt Vera (Again, don't ask me how I know this, I just do. And it's solid intelligence).

"Who is he, Sammy?"

"His name is Robert Moore. He's the new hotshot SAS operator, and he reports directly to the very top Brass. He was especially brought in to eliminate Shepherd's killer and anyone who could connect Shepherd with the killing of Fr. Maguire".

"Does that mean they found out I was in Washington?" Mac Ireland asked.

"No, I don't think they know that. It's probably because you were known to be a close friend of Fr. Maguire, and they want you out of the way so you cannot pursue the case – not to mention all your other activity."

But Sammy, why haven't they gone after you? They must be aware Mrs. Johnson was your aunt. Sure, you were at the funeral and the RUC and the Brits would have been aware of everyone who attended the funeral."

"Oh, I understand that, Patrick. I'm not sure why they haven't gone after me."

"I hope it is not because they hope you will lead them to me."

"Now, Patrick, I hope you realize that I am in as much danger as you…Maybe even more. After all, you are the enemy, and they expect you to do what you do. On the other hand, I am a policeman. I'm supposed to be on their side. If they find out, my death will be particularly vicious. Even worse, they could accuse me of treason and execute me. And that for a loyal Ulster man would be deeply shameful."

"Well, Sammy, let's not write our epitaphs just yet. What do we do? Clearly we have the same mutual interest in taking care of Moore as we did Shepherd. And (here Mac Ireland tried to lighten things bit) we don't have to travel across the Atlantic and live in a monastery."

Johnson smiled: "It may be easier, however, to take him down in America than in The North or The South. Now let me get to what is most on your mind – the British agent in the IRA".

"Guess who his handler is? Yes, yes, the very same – the hotshot Mr. Moore."

"But, Sammy, quit torturing me. Who's the bloody the agent?"

"Your current Chief of Staff. He was turned years ago".

Mac Ireland felt the air go out of his lungs as if Rocky Marciano had punched him in the solar plexus. He bent over in his seat.

It was shocking enough that Emmet Mulligan had been an agent, but that Harry Brogan was also an agent was just too much to take in. Mac Ireland had known the Dublin man for years. He would have trusted him with his life – indeed, often did.

Mac Ireland – still bent over in his chair – was now feeling more pain in his chest than when the bullet proof vest had stopped the two bullets. In all his time in the IRA, he had never received a more shattering blow. He could feel himself getting sick, so he excused himself and darted to the bathroom.

Johnson could hear him vomiting into the toilet bowl. He didn't want Mac Ireland to be embarrassed, so he turned on the TV and waited for Mac Ireland to return.

After twenty minutes, Mac Ireland returned, having washed his teeth and face.

"Man dear, I haven't vomited in over twenty years. I have never been so shaken or horrified. This is unbelievable."

Sammy turned off the TV. "Are you able to discuss strategy, Patrick, or will I go and come back tomorrow?"

"No, no, I'm fine. We must get on with it, Sammy, because time is running out for both of us."

"Here's what I'm thinking, Patrick: The last time, I was able to give you the intelligence on Mulligan's meeting his handler at Carrybridge. That will never work again. They will realize that they have to avoid such meetings. So we have a real impasse."

"Sammy, don't forget one importance difference.

Mulligan was from County Down; therefore, it made sense for them to have the meeting in The North. Harry Brogan is a Dublin man. He would never have crossed the Border to meet anyone in The North. He would have had his meetings over the years in The South. Probably right here in Dublin – just as we are having our meeting."

"Ah ha, Patrick, you may be on to something there. And there must also be another difference when the time comes: you were by yourself at Carrybridge, but this time, I have to be there. The bastard Moore blew my aunt's head off. I have to be involved."

"Yes, Sammy, I understand that. But there is another possible configuration. You could get Moore in the North, and I could get Brogan in The South. That would be much easier than hoping we might get them together. It would require less intelligence.

Johnson recognized the logic of this. "Maybe, that is the way to go," he responded.

"And, Sammy, there is far less risk in it for each of us. You can more easily get Moore in The North, and I can more easily get Brogan here in The South.

Again, Johnson agreed, but queried, "What if I got intelligence that they were meeting in The South? What would we do then?"

Mac Ireland sprang to his feet, apparently totally recovered from his nausea, and declared: "Then we take them together. There would be poetic justice in an SAS assassin and an IRA traitor dying together."

They left it at that – to go with whatever plan would work, and to be in touch.

Johnson left and Mac Ireland got ready for bed. He wondered when he had last slept in a hotel.

CHAPTER 20

The morning after his meeting with Johnson, Mac Ireland was driving back to the Cavan-Fermanagh Border.

He realized, this time, he would have to bring Liam O'Neill in on his plans to deal with the treacherous Chief of Staff. And he was aware that he had now reached the single most dangerous juncture in his life. He could be easily killed by either the Brits or the IRA – or by both working together. Indeed, both – in the person of the IRA Chief of Staff, and in the person of Robert Moore – had already tried to kill him.

Mac Ireland was absolutely under no illusions: if the Chief of Staff sensed for a moment that Mac Ireland was on to him, Mac Ireland would not survive.

For the Chief of Staff to have survived so long under cover as a British agent meant he had not only been exceedingly careful, but that he also had powerful friends. The Chief of Staff could easily arrange for genuine IRA men to execute him, thinking they would be helping the Irish Cause.

"If I go to other members of the IRA Army Council, the Chief of Staff will learn of it, and I will be a dead man," Mac Ireland mused as the car approached Cavan town.

When he was dropped off near Bellturnbet, he got a message to Liam O'Neill to meet him in a safe house that Mac Ireland had not used in over a year.

When O'Neill arrived, Mac Ireland filled him in – flooring him with the revelations. "Patrick, if anyone else but yourself told me that I wouldn't believe it – not even if the Pope himself told me. This is unbelievable – even though I heard Kevin, shortly before he was assassinated, express reservations about Brogan."

O'Neill went silent for a long while. "What are we going to do, Patrick?"

"We have to execute him. And we have to do it just by ourselves. We cannot trust anyone except Sammy Johnson. Liam, I feel bad about bringing you into all this – I am putting your life in danger."

"No, you're not. Harry Brogan is putting all our lives in danger, and threatening everything many good men and women have died for. I am glad you brought me in. And if we are killed, then so be it. It is our duty. We have no other choice."

"Liam, we are going to have to wait awhile until I hear back from Johnson. If we can get Moore and Brogan together in The South, we will take them there. If not, Johnson will have to take care of Moore in The North, and we, Brogan in The South. In the meantime, let's see what information we can pick up on Brogan's next few weeks."

Mac Ireland moved to a safe house near Navan – a safer distance from the Border, and closer to Dublin (yet not too close in case the Dublin-based Brogan was having him watched).

He learned that Brogan was staying for a few weeks

in a hotel in Bray.

In a few days he got a message to call Johnson. He went to a hotel in Navan, and called from a telephone in the lobby.

"I may have something, Patrick." declared Johnson. "Moore has a meeting in Bray in ten days' time."

"Oh, God, that's it."

"What do you mean?"

I have learned that Brogan is staying at a hotel in Bray. That likely means Moore is meeting him."

"Whoa, that does seem likely. However, there's an added twist. A top Special Branch man is going to be with Moore."

"You mean a RUC Special Branch man?"

"No, Patrick, I do not. I mean a Dublin Special Branch man or, as you would say, a 'Free Stater.'"

"Mother of God!" exclaimed Mac Ireland.

"The Special Branch man was recruited by MI5 years ago and has been working since then for the British, and being extremely well paid. He is known to be close to an Irish Government Cabinet Minister. We have opened a real can of worms. I realize this may change everything as I understand the IRA has standing orders against shooting a member of the security forces of the Republic."

"It doesn't change anything. There are no standing orders against shooting British spies, and that's what that bastard is."

"So it's still a go?"

"Yes, now more than ever. But I am going to have to bring in another man on this."

"If you trust him, Patrick, that's good enough for me. And by the way, we don't have to worry about any of the three having security. None of them will want anybody to be aware that they are meeting – not Moore, not Brogan and certainly not the Special Branch man."

"Man, this may not be as difficult as I had anticipated," responded an encouraged Mac Ireland.

They made arrangements to meet two days in advance of the Bray meeting, and at a hotel in Dun Laogharie that Mac Ireland had used before. In that way, they would be literally in striking distance.

Mac Ireland contacted Liam O'Neill and filled him in – telling him to bring two Browning HPs and, just in case, two A47s. He had his own Browning HP with him.

As planned, two days before the Bray meeting, Mac Ireland went up the back stairs of the hotel in Dun Laogharie.

The fourth floor room had been reserved and checked into by one of his trusted contacts. The moment Mac Ireland entered the room, the contact, Mickey, a man in his forties, gave him the keys and left.

Mickey was perhaps a bit odd, but had been helpful. He was originally from Fermanagh, and had known the Mac Irelands all his life. While not an IRA member, he was sympathetic, to a degree. He worked in the hotel business and knew every hotel in the greater Dublin area. Years ago he had told Mac Ireland he would help him in every way to do with the hotel business: free rooms for the night, a place to park his car, etc. etc. – but nothing else. "And one thing more, Patrick, nobody must know about me. I do not trust city people. I will only deal with you, and only at that level of activity. I can get you keys to vacant rooms, etc., but nothing else. I don't want to know anything about your business. You can say I am a "limited" patriot – I have strict parameters, outside of which I will not step."

Mac Ireland settled in. It was a large room, as planned, with two single beds and a roll-a-way-bed. They would keep a low profile. Mickey would bring them food, so they would not have to eat out. Just bread, cheese and apples would keep them going. They could make tea in the room.

Mac Ireland kicked off his shoes picked the bed by the window, leaving the other bed for Johnson. The young Tyrone man could have the roll-a-way bed.

He lay down and napped for twelve minutes.

O'Neill was the first to arrive. He was a bit nervous about meeting Johnson. "The only times I was in the presence of Protestant detectives, they were beating the daylights out of me."

Mac Ireland eased his mind. "Just use your first name. Johnson won't ask you any compromising questions."

Johnson soon arrived wearing black sneakers and a dark running suit with a hood that was turned down.

They exchanged pleasantries and got right down to business.

"I've even got the room number they're meeting in," Johnson announced with relish. "In the morning we can drive into Bray and check out the hotel. This could to be easier than we feared."

He went on to explain that the Special Branch man was called Brian Kelly, originally from Clones, County Monaghan, he was close to fifty, and had spent his entire life in the Special Branch. He was moved up the ranks quickly as he always seemed to have friends in high places. It was likely that he would be armed, and, of course, so would Robert Moore.

"I can't be sure about Brogan. You boys will have a better idea on that."

"We have to assume the bastard will have a gun," cautioned O'Neill.

Mac Ireland nodded his assent. "And talking about guns, Sammy, what did you bring?"

Johnson got up, went to the small travel bag he had put at the bottom of his bed, and produced his weapon.

"It's the standard gun – Ruger Speed Six Revolver-Caliber 357 Magnum – that all detectives in Northern Ireland are given. It's not my own and it's not traceable. I have another one in the bag, and a silencer, plus an automatic shot-gun in the car, and a bullet proof vest."

"And I have most certainly my bullet proof vest, too," chipped in Mac Ireland with a laugh.

"Me, too," affirmed O'Neill.

The following Monday – after having cheese, bread and apples for breakfast, courtesy of Mickey – the three men went to have a look at Harry Brogan's hotel.

Johnson was particularly anxious to find out if the room number he had been told was also Brogan's room number.

Since Brogan knew both Mac Ireland and Liam O'Neill, it was up to Johnson to walk through the inside of the hotel and draw up a floor plan.

The big question was how to burst into the room – whichever room it would be.

Mac Ireland found himself wondering if Mickey could help. After all, the "limited patriot" had promised he could get keys!

The Bray View Hotel was a 60-room building with

a car park in the front and rear. It was just off the main road.

Johnson drove around to the rear parking lot.

"There it is, boys," pointing to the rear entrance. Sit here while I check it out."

And off he went.

"We'll be in some mess if Brogan walks out and sees us," observed O'Neill.

"He probably doesn't move much out of the hotel," assured Mac Ireland.

In twenty minutes Johnson was back.

"I saw the room. Of course, I can't be sure who's in it. It is on the second floor, and it's at the end of the corridor. Best of all, it's right beside an exit door which leads to stairs that come out over there," pointing to the left of the building. "Now let's move away from here."

On the way back to their own hotel, Johnson declared, "The real issue is how do we break into the room in the middle of their meeting? The doors seemed quite strong. At the front desk I saw some room keys – really big, which means the locks are old style and secure."

"What if I can get a spare key?" asked Mac Ireland.

"Oh, boy, then we are in business," replied Johnson.

"Drive along about half a mile until we come to a big hotel on the right," Mac Ireland directed. "Let me make a call from the lobby. What was that room number, again, Sammy?"

"212."

"Okay, I'll be right back."

Mac Ireland found a phone in the lobby, dialed a number, and spoke to Mickey for a couple of minutes, then hung up.

Back in the car, he announced with relish: "Gentlemen, we will have a spare key to room 212 by 9 P.M. this evening."

"Now we are in business, boys," Johnson rejoiced.

CHAPTER 21

Back at their hotel room, the three of them got down to serious plans.

Johnson, with remarkable ability, sketched out a detailed floor plan.

"Gosh, Sammy, you could have been an architect," observed O'Neill.

"Always wanted to be," replied Johnson.

Johnson's intelligence information had revealed that the meeting of Moore, Brogan and Kelly would be at 10P.M. He wasn't sure if Moore and Kelly had also planned to spend the night in the hotel. "But if we do our job, they certainly won't be leaving," he hissed.

"Now, let's discuss the actual logistics of the room invasion," Johnson continued. "I have more experience in kicking down doors – done hundreds in West Belfast," he added slyly.

"Well don't try that in Tyrone, buckhoo," snapped O'Neill.

Johnson paused and stared at O'Neill, not too sure how he should take the riposte.

They were losing focus for a moment.

Mac Ireland jumped in, "Steady up boys. Stay the

course. Sammy, please continue."

"Alright, if it's okay with you both, I suggest I take the lead on this. I know what Moore looks like whereas you guys don't. And I know what Brogan looks like. Here's what we do: The door opens to the left (the front desk had a brochure with photos of the rooms). I enter quickly, go to the left past the bathroom, the bed is here (and he sketched out the location) and the table and chairs are here (again, showing off his sketching skills). The moment I go in, leaving room for you, Patrick, to follow, I will shoot Moore. Patrick, you shoot Brogan and Liam, you simultaneously shoot Kelly. Remember, he is certain to be armed like Moore. If it goes according to plans, it should be quite simple. We should be able to do it with a minimum of fuss. Just be sure, Liam, that you close the door behind you when you've entered the room. We should be able to leave the hotel without anyone even knowing there was a shooting. Hopefully, we will all be home – those of us who have homes – (he smiled knowingly) before the bodies are discovered."

Mac Ireland got up and walked around the room. (He was hopeful he would be well on his way to his wife in France when the bodies were discovered.). Then he turned to the other two: "We will be leaving the AK-47s and the shotgun, in the car. I hate to think we might have to use them on the way out of the parking lot as that could endanger civilians. Hopefully, as you pointed out, Sammy, them boys are not going to have any back up."

"No, it won't come to that, Patrick," assured Johnson. There's no way the Special Branch man wants the Guards to find out he is meeting the Chief of Staff of the IRA. And there's no way Brogan wants the IRA to know he's meeting with either the SAS or Special Branch. These guys have hoisted themselves on their own petard. Deceit and deception are their own undoing."

"How do we leave the hotel room when the deed is done?" asked O'Neill, "together or separately?"

"The room is right beside the exit," Johnson explained. "We just exit quickly in single file. And since each of us will be wearing wigs, it doesn't really matter if anyone sees us. At that time of night, nobody will be paying much attention. I drive you guys back to the hotel and I head back to Belfast."

At 9 P.M. on the dot, there was a knock on the door.

"I'll get it," volunteered Mac Ireland as he sprang up.

Mickey was at the door with a key that almost looked the size of a small hammer.

"By the way," he disclosed, "the man in room 212 has been there over a week... He's registered as James Duffy."

"Thanks, Mickey."

When he closed the door, Mac Ireland announced to the other two, "Yes, it's Brogan who's staying in room 212. He's been there over a week."

Things were now falling nicely in place. The three men kicked back a bit and began to relax.

Shortly they got ready for bed. This night, Mac Ireland would not kneel to say his to say his prayers, saying them in bed, instead.

The following day, they rehearsed the details of the operation – over and over again. Got lots of sleep and mentally prepared for the action that would bring swift and terrible justice.

They had decided not to go to the Bray View Hotel until after 10 P.M, as not to attract possible attention from either Kelly or Moore.

At 10:15, they were parked right beside the entrance to the stairs that lead to room 212. They donned their amazingly effective wigs, which totally changed their appearances and put on their gloves. Led by Johnson, they climbed the stairs to the second floor. The corridor was empty. Johnson, with the large key in his right hand, looked at the other two and nodded as if to say, "Okay, men, this is it."

Then he inserted the key, turned it silently, put the key in his left hand, grabbed his revolver in his right hand, and stepped into the room and commanded, "Nobody move."

Harry Brogan was sitting behind the small table and was facing the door. Moore was to his left and Kelly to the right. All three scrambled wildly and awkwardly to their feet.

Brogan, a small rumpled man, yelled in his real Dublin accent, "Jaysus, what the hell!"

"I told you not to move," barked Johnson, shooting Robert Moore right in the chest and then in the head.

Simultaneously, Brogan went down, blown backwards by Mac Ireland's shot to the heart, followed by one to the head.

Brian Kelly had succeeded in getting his right hand on his pistol, holstered under his left arm, when O'Neill's two bullets blew the life out of his traitorous body.

Then they silently left the room. Johnson, the last out, calmly locked the door taking the key with him. They climbed into their car, not having seen a living soul.

Johnson calmly drove out of the parking lot.

Back at their hotel parking lot, O'Neill took the AK7s out of Johnson's car and put them in his own. He shook hands with Johnson. Then Mac Ireland said: "Sammy, I hope your son, Billy, and your Aunt Vera can now rest in peace. And I hope we don't have to meet again – either as friends or enemies."

"Indeed," Johnson replied, affirming the serious import of Mac Ireland's words. Then he sped off to Belfast, safely dumping the hotel key miles from Dublin.

O'Neill drove Mac Ireland to a safe house on the back road into Dublin.

"Liam, I will be out of touch for a while. You, too, should lie low for a few weeks."

They exchanged good-byes.

In the safe house, Mac Ireland grabbed his pre-packed bag, "Let's go, Oliver."

Oliver O'Shea drove Mac Ireland south through Bray again, onto Wicklow, ending in Rosslare Harbor. There Mac Ireland spent a restful night in a local hotel waiting for his boat to the continent the following evening – sailing overnight.

After eighteen hours, he arrived in Roscoff, where once Bonnie Prince Charlie and Mary Queen of Scots had landed.

On the dock, brimming with excitement was Mrs. Mary McDonough-Mac Ireland.

The establishment Irish and British media tried to cover up the Bray killing. First, they announced authoritatively that it was a gangland slaying – a drug feud.

Then a few committed journalists exposed that one of the slain men was a top Dublin Special Branch man. Later, it got out that another of the dead men was the Chief of Staff of the IRA. And then all hell broke loose when the third man was revealed to be top a SAS man.

Even the media that historically had covered up so much for the British Government had to admit, "This potentially was a most serious state of affairs."

"And it will get even more serious," pledged Mac Ireland from his place of refuge in France. "I pledge Her Majesty's government that!" he whispered as he made plans to return to Ireland and continue the fight for freedom. Yet, he had the nagging feeling that he may have had his last-pitched battle with the British army in the field ... That when he shortly returned to Ireland, his major battle would be to rid his beloved IRA of British agents.

CHAPTER 22

Mac Ireland soon made plans to return to Ireland. Mary's French friends made arrangements for him to fly on a small private plane into Shannon Airport.

He immediately made contact with his Second in Command of the Cavan-Fermanagh IRA, Liam O'Neill. They met in a safe house outside Virginia, County Cavan.

"Patrick, it's getting real tough to operate along the South Fermanagh border. The Brits are very heavy on the ground. And the Free State Army and Special Branch are colluding with them very closely."

"What's the general reaction to the execution (our execution) of the Chief of Staff of the IRA, Harry Brogan?"

"At first there was shock and disbelief that he was a British agent. But now there is universal acceptance that the bastard was an agent. And they are all glad we got him – but they still do not know you and I were involved."

"Good. We must keep it that way because it is certain that Brogan was not the only agent at the top of the IRA and we may have to take care of him, or them, too."

"Good, Patrick. And please involve me, again, in any such action. Unless we eradicate all British agents, our Movement will be destroyed. They know they can't beat us from outside, so they will try to do it from the inside."

"Don't worry, Liam. I will keep you involved. Right now you are the only one I can trust in this role. Head back now to the Cavan border, activate all the IRA units, but don't tell them anything about my movements or our conversation."

O'Neill quickly exited. Twenty minutes later, Mac Ireland got ready to leave. He checked around the small, neatly furnished living room to make sure everything was in order. He lifted his brief case, which was a key part of his disguise ensemble. It was remarkable that nobody seemed to expect a countryman like himself – the son of a poor, small farmer – to carry a brief case. Though he was aware it would not fool British Intelligence and the dreaded SAS.

Opening the door, Mac Ireland stepped into the cool Cavan evening air. As he turned around to lock the door, the upper class English accent hissed: "Die, you Irish bastard."

Mac Ireland had only a split second to see the Browning HP, single action, 9mm semi-automatic pistol pointing at his head. He froze, knowing it was all over. But all he heard was a dull sound as the Browning HP jammed. He smashed the assassin's gun-hand with the hard edge of the brief case, knocking the pistol to the ground. Then with all the power of his right foot – strengthened over the years by playing GAA football – he kicked the SAS assassin ferociously in the groin, picked up the pistol and, praying it would not jam again, pulled the trigger. The blast caught the English assassin in the chest as he straightened up from the kick in the groin. It smashed him flat on his back. Mac Ireland calmly walked toward the sprawled killer and shot him again in the head – to make sure he would never again be dispatched by Her Majesty's Government to kill innocent civilians or Irish freedom fighters like himself.

Knowing that the killer most likely had not come alone, Mac Ireland dashed back into the house and locked the door, dived on his belly and crawled on his elbows into the kitchen. He knew if there were an SAS patrol outside, there was no way he could get through the front or back door (an SAS patrol usually has four soldiers). Furthermore, even if the SAS had slithered away having illegally invaded the alleged sovereign territory of the 26 county (Irish Republic) – the Irish police (the Guards) and the Free State Amy (the Irish Army) would soon be arriving on the scene.

Once in the kitchen, Mac Ireland felt free to stand up – the kitchen having no window. He grabbed hold of the no longer used heating-cooking stove, twisted it sideways, sliding it smoothly on its well-greased tracks – revealing a tunnel underneath. He scampered down the hole, pulling the range back into its place.

The tunnel – which his IRA Unit had dug six years previously – was five feet down. Mac Ireland reached down and grabbed around in the pitch darkness until his hand felt the torch (flash light) that he knew would be there.

Turning on the torch, he bent over and quickly scurried along the well-made tunnel. After four hundred yards, the tunnel came to an end – with a four-rung wooden ladder pointing to the roof.

Mac Ireland stepped on the second rung, raised his two hands above his head and pushed on the trap door that opened with minimum pressure. Stepping on the third rung, and on the fourth, he rolled onto the floor of a hayshed, which was totally enclosed and windowless.

Mac Ireland – still using the light from his torch – closed the trap door, rolled over it a wooden trestle, which he then covered with twenty bales of hay. (A far cry from when he and his father used to "ruck" hay – build stacks of hay in the fields with pitch forks.).

Then Mac Ireland slid a steel bolt on a narrow side door of the hay shed, walked across a small patch of ground, and knocked on the back door of the farmhouse.

A tall, scholarly looking man in his early seventies opened the door.

"Ah, Patrick, it's yourself."

"Yes, Roger, and you have to get me out of here right away."

"Let me get the car keys, Patrick, and we will be on the road right away."

Roger was the pharmacist (chemist). More importantly, however, he was a member of a prominent Fine Gael family in the area, and, therefore, above suspicion. The Fine Gael Party was seen as stridently anti -IRA. Still, there were always some party members who actually believed in the subtitle that accompanied their official title – "Fine Gael: the United Ireland Party."

The patriotic Roger Brady felt he was being true to the legacy of Michael Collins (1890-1922) by providing safe passage to Mac Ireland. Fine Gael looked to Collins as their leader, whereas the other main party, Fianna Fail, looked to Eamon De Valera (1882-1975).

Within two hours, Mac Ireland was dropped off at a safe house just a couple of miles from the South Fermanagh border.

CHAPTER 23

The following day, Liam O'Neill came to see Mac Ireland.

"Patrick, how did the Brits know you were in the safe house? Do you think they were there while I was leaving? I wonder why they didn't assassinate me. Jaysus, Patrick, you don't think I had any part in setting you up?"

"Easy there, Liam. Of course, I know you didn't set me up. As I told you in that safe house, you are the only one I can trust in the role of helping me to eliminate the British agents at the very top of the IRA. If we are ever going to get the Brits out of Ireland, we must first get them out of the IRA.

"What are we going to do, Patrick? There seems to be no end to Brit penetration of our Movement politically and militarily."

"Isn't it pathetic, Liam, that we have to spend more time fighting the British agents in the IRA than fighting the British Army in the field, so to speak? I should really go and meet with the IRA Army Council. But the second last time I did that, your brother Kevin and I were ambushed and Kevin was killed. ... So, I am reluctant to do that again."

"Yet, Patrick, if you do not meet the Army Council, they will wonder why. Do you know the new chief of staff who took Harry Brogan's place?"

"Yes, I know him – it's Sean O'Connell, a Corkman. He soldiered with my brother Terence, God rest him, in the 1956 Campaign. He's a good man and there is no way that he is a British Agent."

"Well, Patrick, why don't you go and talk to him privately?"

"Yes, I just might do that. If I cannot trust him, then I cannot trust any of the other six men on the Army Council. I will try to make contact with Sean and go and see him. I'll be in touch in a few days."

Mac Ireland said good-bye and left the safe house.

The following day, Mac Ireland headed for Bundoran in County Donegal, driven by his driver, Peader Sheridan.

O'Connell who was staying in a safe house just about half a mile outside of Bundoran on the main Enniskillen road.

As Mac Ireland entered the house, O'Connell immediately said, "Good disguise, Patrick," referring to Mac Ireland's brown, curly wig, and round-rim eyeglasses.

"Your own make-up is pretty good, too, Sean." The two friends shook hands, glad to see each other.

O'Connell was 6'2", rail thin, dark and handsome in a haggard, almost sickly way.

In the 1956 campaign, he was riddled with British bullets while being ambushed in Northern Ireland, and his health had never really recovered. But that would not stop this intrepid Corkman. He had kept the Fenian faith and had gone on to be one of the most respected men in

The Movement.

O'Connell had great charm and a compelling Cork accent. However, he was an absolutely formidable man with nerves of steel and an iron will. And he could be quite ruthless. Mac Ireland liked and admired him.

O'Connell didn't wait for Mac Ireland to begin.

"Patrick, I want you on the Army Council with me.

"No, Sean, I am not going on it. I don't know whom I can trust."

"Join the Army Council, Patrick, and help me purge all British Agents that may be on the Council."

"But, Sean, there are already seven members on the Council. There is no room for me on it."

"That's no problem, Patrick. Michael McGreevy from Clare is in poor health, and wants to step down. Furthermore, it is just too dangerous for you to be anywhere near The Border because the Brits are determined to kill you. You are just too important to The Cause to take any further, unnecessary chances. If the Brits killed you, it would be an enormous blow to the morale of The Movement.

"Sean, I appreciate your confidence in me. Let me think about it, and talk to my South Fermanagh Unit."

"Here's the thing, Patrick," (And suddenly, O'Connell's charm was replaced by resolute determination.). "I don't want to pull rank on you. But whether or not you agree to join me on the Army Council, I am pulling you away from The Border. It is just too risky for you, and I cannot, as Chief-of-Staff, allow it."

"If I'm not on the Border where will I be based? If I do go on the Army Council, what would I be doing?"

"We may have to send you to America, Patrick. There are some problems there among our supporters, and you are the man to sort them out. Plus, we need to get you to a safe area, at least for a time."

"Sean, with respect, I think it's not the time for me to go to America even for a short time. Our Movement is compromised at the very top. First, it was Emmet Mulligan, given his just desserts when someone killed him at Carrybridge, Co. Fermanagh. And then our former Chief of Staff, Harry Brogan, killed in Bray while meeting a SAS man and or Free State (Irish Government) Special Branch man." (Mac Ireland did not mention that he was the one who had executed Mulligan or that he, Liam O'Neill and the Northern Ireland Protestant Detective, Sammy Johnson, had executed the other three men.).

Mac Ireland added: "Sean, if we don't finish the British agents at the top of the IRA, they will finish not just me, but they will destroy the IRA from within.

O'Connell was now giving his famous stare – as if he was looking straight through Mac Ireland.

"What do you think I should do, Patrick?"

"Put me in charge of tracking down the British Agents at the center of the IRA and appoint Liam O'Neill as my Number 2. I will get someone to run the South Fermanagh Unit while Liam and I are on this special assignment."

O'Connell lit another cigarette. Unlike Mac Ireland, he had never stopped smoking – the habit no doubt contributing to his sickly pallor.

"Okay, Patrick, I give you and Liam that appointment. It's best if we keep it strictly between the three of us.

You will have all the funds and support you need. Be careful, for you are a marked man."

"I know," Mac Ireland responded. "In fact, I am convinced the Brits want me dead to stop me hunting down their agents in the IRA – and not just because our South Fermanagh Unit has exacted heavy casualties on the British Army. Their agents have always been more important to the British Government than their soldiers."

"You're quite right there, Patrick. The British counter insurgency against the IRA has mostly been an intelligence operation – placing agents in The Movement, buying information, paying informers, etc."

"Indeed, Sean. My father always said: "Fear not the man in uniform, but fear the man out of uniform."

Then Mac Ireland stood up, shook hands with O'Connell and went off to where his driver was waiting in the car.

CHAPTER 24

Mac Ireland chatted with his driver, Peadar Sheridan, on the way back from Bundoran. But as always, he kept a wary eye out for any cars that may be following him.

He had told his driver to stay well away from the Border. So they had driven to Sligo town and were on their way to Drumshanbo – intending to cut across to Balinamore and then into Cavan town.

Two miles before Drumshambo, Mac Ireland noticed a car coming up behind very rapidly. At first, he feared another ambush, but suddenly the car had flashing lights and a siren. Mac Ireland felt relief to be quickly replaced by concern! Free State Special Branch – in an unmarked car – could never be a cause for rejoicing.

Mac Ireland then told his driver to obey the siren and pull over. The special Branch man came to the passenger side of the car, opened the door, flashed an identification card and told Mac Ireland to step out of the car – and ordered the driver to keep going. The driver took off cursing Free State traitors under his breath. As he watched the driver take off, Mac Ireland wasn't sure if his was just a nuisance arrest, petty harassment or even abduction with assassination to follow. After all, just a few moments ago, he, Liam O'Neill and Sammy

Johnson had executed a top Special Branch man, Brian Kelly, who was working for the British.

Mac Ireland looked closely at the Special Branch man: he was in his late 30s, about 5'10", full head of sandy hair with open, friendly features.

Smiling at Mac Ireland, the Special Branch man said, "Relax. I come in peace! Despite your disguise, I know who you are, Patrick."

Mac Ireland was not expecting this. "Please, come with me in the car, Patrick, I want to talk to you – well away from prying eyes. Don't fret, I mean you no harm."

Eyeing him cautiously, Mac Ireland followed him and got into the car.

"I am going to drive a few miles down the road to a quiet spot where we can talk."

Mac Ireland nodded. The car pulled off the road onto an isolated dirt road. The Special Branch man switched off the engine, and turned toward Mac Ireland, and held out his hand.

"I'm Mick Duffy. You knew my great-aunt Lizzie Duffy in Kincally parish. My grandfather moved from Kincally many years ago and I was born in Sligo town."

Mac Ireland shook his hand, felt himself relaxing, but still remaining cautious.

"I remember Lizzie fondly, Mick. She was a lovely woman. And (here he couldn't help but rub in it) if memory serves, she was an ardent Irish Republican."

Duffy smiled, accepting the implied rebuke.

"Okay, okay, Patrick. Don't get on your Republican high horse. I am here to help."

"Why would a Free State Special Branch man help the likes of me?"

"Because there is deep disgust and shame among some of us that one of us, Brian Kelly, was working for the British. And we are glad the IRA executed him. I want to eliminate British agents from the Special Branch – just as I am sure you want to eliminate them from the IRA."

Mac Ireland stared intently at Duffy beginning to think that old Lizzie Duffy would have been quite proud of her grand nephew. Nonetheless, he declared with great seriousness, and low-keyed intensity: "Mick, if you are for real, you must realize the seriousness of what you are doing, and if you are not (and instead are trying to trick me), then I ASSURE you of the seriousness of your actions."

"I am perfectly clear on both accounts, Patrick. I know I am putting both my career and life on the line."

Mac Ireland sat in silence, carefully weighing up his new unexpected ally. When it was clear his silence was beginning to make Duffy uneasy, he said, "Okay, Mick, what do you think you can do to help?"

"I think the number two Special Branch man, Michael Flynn – the Kerry man who really runs the Special Branch – is also a British agent. I can prove it, but not in a Court of Law because the Government would never allow it. And if I move against him through the ordinary channels, I will be squashed like a bug and drummed out of the Special Branch in disgrace."

"How can you prove it?"

"Because I was based for two years at the Dublin Headquarters, I got suspicious of him. Followed him on a few occasions, even photographed him secretly meeting people whom I think were Brits – MI5 or SAS."

"Can I see your evidence, Mick?"

"Sure you can. I have it safely stashed away in a safety box in a bank. I can retrieve it within three days and meet with you in Dublin, a week from today."

"Let's do it. But Mick, you must now get me back to the Cavan town area. We have been here long enough. We should move before someone sees us."

"Okay, Patrick, we're off. But, by the way, what will your driver have told people about my stopping you?"

"Don't worry; he knows not to say anything to anybody until I speak to him. That's why he is my driver."

CHAPTER 25

Liam O'Neill had just finished supervising a huge supply of weapons to the Fermanagh-Cavan IRA. Most of the weapons were hidden along the Cavan border, but some were rather ingeniously hidden across the Border in Fermanagh on Protestant farms where the Brits would never think of searching.

When he got the message that Mac Ireland wanted to see him immediately, O'Neill couldn't wait to get there. This time, Mac Ireland was in a safe house in Mullingar, and O'Neill made it there in good time.

"How would you like to be my Number 2 on a new mission?" Mac Ireland immediately asked. And proceeded to fill him in on all the details – the meeting with the new Chief-of-Staff, Sean O'Connell, and the strange meeting with the Special Branch man.

O'Neill was visibly excited: "Jaysus, Patrick, this is great. It needs to be done. And we are the two men who can do it."

Mac Ireland was delighted, but not the least surprised by O'Neill's generous and willing response.

"Liam, we've got to say good-bye for a while to our combat fatigues, and AK-47s. We have to change our entire modus operandi. We are going to be operating in cities, not by the Fermanagh-Cavan Mountains, and we have to act as executives rather than soldiers. There's a fancy, very large house waiting for us in Dublin. We have a team of drivers and safe cars. And The Movement has provided us with all the money we need. O'Connell has guaranteed us every possible support – only a few people will know our true function."

Mac Ireland had previously confided to O'Neill about his secret marriage to Mary. And he then continued to explain that Mary – who was on her way back from France – would be living at the house. Well, at least, part of the time.

"Now, Liam, go back to the Border, meet with the Fermanagh-Cavan IRA. And tell them I've appointed Jimmy Mc Govern as the acting O.C. with young Eamon Mc Nally as second in command. We must be in our Dublin residence within the week."

O'Neill headed for the Border, and Mac Ireland was driven to Dublin City. His driver dropped Mac Ireland off at his new residence on Orwell Road, a very swanky section of Dublin. The house was most impressive. Totally walled off with extensive ground. It was three stories: had three bathrooms, six rooms, large study/ library and big sitting room and huge kitchen. Best of all, it was really secure and private. Nobody would ever expect that two of the most wanted IRA men from The North would be quite cheekily residing there – hiding in plain sight.

Among the keys given to Mac Ireland was a key to the safe. Inside the safe were two hundred fifty thousand Irish punts in small bills, and the same amount in British pounds, small and used.

Mac Ireland assumed name would be Pat Mullen and his wife would be Mary Mullen. His cover job would be real estate. People tended to lose interest when they were told one was "in real estate." O'Neill would go by the name of Liam O'Reilly, and he, too, would be in real estate.

Mac Ireland contacted Mick Duffy, Special Branch, and gave him the address of the house where he could go to the meeting.

Exactly a week from their first meeting outside Drumshambo, Mac Ireland welcomed Duffy to the residence, and he explained that Liam O'Neill (aka O'Reilly) would take part in the meeting.

After brief introductions, O'Neill and Duffy sat down and Mac Ireland said, "Let's see your evidence, Mick."

Duffy went to the TV set, turned it on and popped a video into the VCR.

At first, the video was a bit grainy and fuzzy, but it soon cleared up. A burly, curly-haired "black" Irishman appeared. "That's the Kerry man, Michael Flynn, the number two Special Branch man in the country," Duffy explained.

"Not in the country. In the 26-County State," snapped O'Neill.

"Never mind, Mick. Tyrone boys can be very touchy. Carry on," Mac Ireland directed.

Duffy continued, a little unnerved by O'Neill's sharp interjection: "Next, you will see Flynn secretly meeting three men in a pub in Drogheda. I have not been able to identify them, but I have no doubt they are Brits."

The picture was pretty clear – Flynn chatting in an animated fashion to two men, with one man in the background. Mac Ireland grabbed the arms of his chair and whispered, "Lord, I can't believe it. Look who's on the right."

It was Charlie Shepherd.

"When did you make this video?" Mac Ireland demanded of Duffy.

"About two years ago."

Mac Ireland was at first amazed that neither Duffy nor O'Neill recognized the infamous assassin of the Kincally priest, Fr. Maguire. And then quickly realized that, in keeping with British policy, no photo of Shepherd had been released. And, furthermore, it had never been made public that Mac Ireland and the Northern Protestant Detective, Sammy Johnson, had executed Shepherd on the National Mall in Washington.

And to complete the picture: on the left was the Brit handler of the IRA traitor, Emmet Mulligan. Both of whom Mac Ireland had executed at Carrybridge, County Fermanagh.

As the picture was freezed on the TV, Mac Ireland got up and paced around the room. "My God, there's no end to this," he exclaimed.

"And that's not all," O'Neill chipped in, "Do either of you recognize the third man in the background?"

Both Mac Ireland and Duffy shook their heads.

"Well, I recognize the bastard," O'Neill hissed. "It's the quartermaster of the Belfast IRA – Chris Gaffney."

Then Duffy said, "Now I want you to listen to a tape recording I made of Flynn talking on the phone to a man in Northern Ireland a short time ago."

He pulled a tape recorder from his brief case and turned it on. Flynn was fairly shouting into the phone: "If

I'm to continue risking my career, I need more money. You've got to pay me at least a half million a year. I've got some of the key Dublin politicians in my pocket. I've blackmailed a number of the key TV and press reporters on Northern Ireland."

The distinctly English accent says, "Michael, I'm sure that can be arranged. Just tell me your latest information."

"Okay, Mr. Hodgetts, if you get MI5-MI6 to increase my pay, I will continue. In the meantime, I can tell you that we suspect that a Northern Ireland detective by the name of Sammy Johnson has been working with your nemesis, Patrick Mac Ireland. They are from the same part of the country, you know, Kincally, on the Cavan border."

The tape ended there. "Whoa, this is unbelievable," O'Neill muttered.

"It's the tape that convinced me I had to contact you, Patrick," Duffy declared. "I remembered my Great Aunt Lizzy spoke highly of the Protestant Johnson family of Kincally. Furthermore, I am convinced Flynn would not be doing this without a wink and a nod from some powerful Dublin politicians – in the main parties. I think they, too, have been bought off by the Brits."

Coming from a Special Branch man, that was serious stuff.

Mac Ireland stopped pacing around the room. He rubbed his left hand down his face (his fake eye glasses not being in place) grabbed his neck and whisked his hand sharply off to the left – as if he were wiping off sweat. It was one of his trademark gestures when under pressure. He walked closer to O'Neill and announced, "We've got to see Sammy Johnson much sooner than we expected. He's in danger and we must get him to come and meet us here."

"Absolutely," affirmed O'Neill.

"Will Johnson be able to find out who this Mr. Hodgetts is?" inquired Duffy.

"Hopefully," Mac Ireland replied. "Well, I think we can end the meeting here. Mick, place your evidence in a safe place. And watch your back. You have now entered a very dangerous stage in your life."

Duffy shook hands with Mac Ireland and O'Neill, and took his leave from the very upscale residence.

The following morning, Mac Ireland took a taxi into Dublin center just to walk around. He found himself outside Leinster House, and stood around with others watching the Free State Politicians come and go.

"I wonder how many of them have sold out for 'the lure of English gold,'" he thought to himself.

As if on cue, Gerald Fitzgarret shuffled by in his busy, self-important way, attended by an obsequious aide. Fitzgarret was – unbelievably, in Mac Ireland's view – one of the most powerful politicians in Southern Ireland. The compliant media loved him; he was anti-Republican, fanatically anti-IRA and a pseudo-intellectual – tailored made for most of the Dublin media.

As Mac Ireland watched Fitzgarret strut along, he reflected on what Mick Duffy had said the night before: that Special Branch men like Michael Flynn could not be working for British Intelligence without the support and protection of politicians like Fitzgarret. "Fitzgarret wouldn't even have to be paid by the Brits," Mac Ireland mused to himself. He is so obsessed with proving Republicans wrong that he would work free for the Brits. Indeed, maybe not even think that he was working for them, so great is his anti-Republican bitterness. He may even think it is his patriotic duty to conspire with the Brits to defeat the IRA.

As Mac Ireland watched the politicians come and go, he spotted another "usual suspect."

Again, another useless Irishman, but like Fitzgarret, promoted incredibly by the media – Seamus O'Lynch.

O'Lynch was a famed hurler, but a useless Irishman. Scared of the Brits, only interested in political survival and good Irish whisky. "These hoors live high on the hog while young men and women are risking their lives every day in The North." Mac Ireland fumed to himself. "In another, self-respecting country, they would be hounded out of office – if not tried for treason. These are the cowardly bastards that have always sold out poor Ireland."

Mac Ireland felt himself literally getting hot under his collar. He knew he would have to move on; he did not want to risk drawing attention to himself. Of course, another reason he may have been feeling hot under his collar was because it was crisp and starched, set-off by a red power tie that completed his "banker" look – blue suit and blue shirt.

As he headed toward the Shelbourne Hotel, he walked right past close neighbors from Kincally – a man and wife with their two teen-age girls. None of them recognized him, and that greatly assured Mac Ireland that his disguise was perfect.

When he entered the lobby of the Shelbourne, Mac Ireland headed for the nearest phone. He dialed the Belfast number, "You need to come immediately," he informed Sammy Johnson and then hung up the phone.

CHAPTER 26

Three days later at 8 P.M., Sammy Johnson knocked on the door of "Mr. Mullen's" swanky abode on Orwell Road.

"Come on in, Sammy," said Mac Ireland as he shook his hand.

Inside, waiting for their unknown ally were Liam O'Neill (AKA O'Reilly), and Mick Duffy.

"You already know Liam," said Mac Ireland to Sammy, waiting while they shook hands. "Now meet your opposite number in the Free State Special Branch."

"That's Irish Republic," interrupted Johnson – all smiles.

"As I was saying," Mac Ireland continued, ignoring the interruption, "this is Mick Duffy, Dublin Special Branch."

Mac Ireland couldn't help but feel quite emotional as he watched the two detectives warmly shake hands – one sworn to uphold The North, the other The South; one Protestant, the other Catholic. Brought together, however, by their sense of justice – disgusted by what the Two-State Ireland had brought into being. Such government corruption had been inevitable to Mac Ireland's mind, but he realized that it had to come as a severe shock to these two detectives. What an extraordinary turn of events when they now had to turn to the IRA for justice to eliminate government evil doing. Mac Ireland glanced quickly at O'Neill knowing that the very same thoughts were flooding his Tyrone mind.

"Sit down, men," Mac Ireland said. "We have to plan our next moves."

END OF BOOK ONE

Made in the USA
Charleston, SC
17 June 2013